FREE FALL

A DOWNFALL PREQUEL NOVELLA

SHAE SCOTT

Sometimes, if you're lucky, you can spot a life changing moment as it happens. It's an instant tingle that shoots through your body, a subtle shift in the air that lets you know this one tiny sliver of time will change everything. You stand up straighter; you snap a picture with your mind so that every detail is committed to memory. Because you know. You know that this moment is special, even if you can't explain why.

When it came to Miles Harris, I didn't have that moment.

But I should have.

That's not to say I didn't notice him. I stood back and stared at him as he moved through the crowds of people in that hotel hallway, itching to follow him. He seemed so out of place, in the middle of this book convention, yet he moved with confidence. He had swagger, like he knew exactly where he was going and exactly what he would do when he got there. I couldn't help but take in the way his tall, powerful body moved as he shifted the weight of the box he carried, or the way his dark hair fell just shy of his honey brown eyes. He smiled at each person in his path, warm and genuine, and it made me want to throw myself on the floor in front of him, so he'd have to stop and talk to me too.

"Lily! There you are. Let's go. We're going to be late for the panel. I want to get a good seat," Quinn, my best friend, tugs at my arm, pulling me from my fantasy. The one where I follow my handsome stranger and convince him to help me find a secluded supply closet. I wonder what his voice sounds like. It's probably deep and sultry.

"Lily," Quinn says again, tugging a little harder.

"Sorry, I got distracted," I laugh.

"You're always distracted," Quinn points out. Quinn has been my best friend since we were kids. We're opposites in a lot of ways. I accuse her of being too careful, she accuses me of being too reckless. I like to think we balance each other out.

She pulls me down the hall, excitement in her eyes as she looks down at the paper in her hand. This week is her graduation present from her parents. A weeklong book convention in San Francisco full of author panels, reader mixers and even a few educational panels on publishing, which is something Quinn wants to work her way into. This trip is basically her dream come true. Mine too, really. We've been reading love stories since before we knew anything about love.

Sometimes I think all that happily ever after stunted our emotional growth. She's too picky, and I'm not nearly picky enough. But give us a good book boyfriend and we're happy girls. Book boyfriends always get it right.

I link my arm with Quinn's, and we move through the halls looking for the next item on our schedule. "Where to next?" I ask her as she consults the week's bible. I mean agenda.

"New Adult: A Look at College Love," Quinn says. Her voice catches as I yank her to a halt. Dark and Handsome is standing at the elevator. Now is my chance.

"There he is. Hold on, I want to say hi," I say cutting her off. I let go of Quinn and merge through the people. Ahead, I can see the elevator door open and my mystery guy steps out of sight. I'm about to bolt forward and hold the doors when a woman calls out, stepping forward. I see his hand reach out to hold the door open.

"Miles, hold the door."

I frown. The woman is beautiful. Stunning. She disappears and the doors close, taking them away, and I let out a huff.

Damn.

At least I got his name this time.

Miles. I like it.

"Did you seriously just leave me to chase after some random guy?" Quinn asks, half irritated and half amused. She's used to me by now, but that doesn't mean she understands me.

"It wasn't some random guy. It was Miles," I say, letting his name roll off my tongue, getting acquainted with it.

"Who is Miles?" she asks.

I shrug and give her a wicked smile, "I don't know. But I plan to find out."

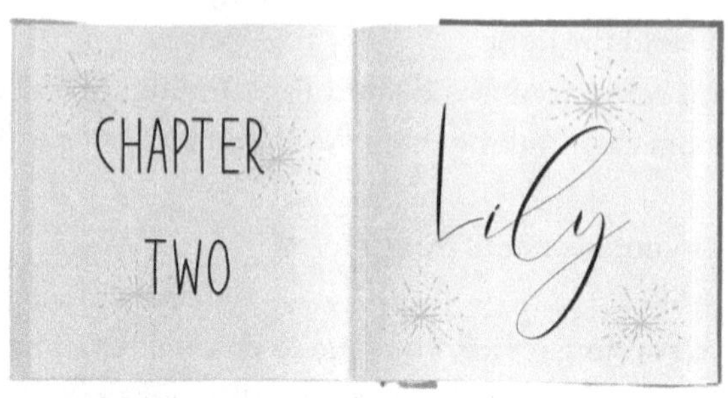

etting lost in the world of a book convention is easy for a pair of book nerds like Quinn and me. We're like two kids in a candy store, suckers for pretty words that rip our hearts out and then piece them back together again. It's our thing. And this place is perfect because we're surrounded by like minds. The people who get it. Who understand what reading is about. Who understand why sometimes you want to stay at home on a Saturday night with a book or why you always have your kindle in your purse in case you get caught somewhere with extra time on your hands.

There's nothing like the emotional journey of a good book. The way you give yourself over to the experience. It's different from a movie or a tv show, with those you're just an observer. With a book, you become part of a new world. You invest your heart and soul into the characters and the places. You feel all the emotions, in some ways you become the characters. You live different lives. You get to have so many experiences. It's part of what makes me want to chase after real-life adventures.

When we stumbled into my mom's old stash of Harlequin romance novels, well, we fell in love with love too. At least the kind we find in books. Quinn believes fairytales only exist in the pages of fiction and I tend to agree with her. I just think it's fun to look for something that might be close enough.

I'm not looking for a happy ending, I like to live in the

buildup. I like to keep things easy and fresh. If you avoid the heavy, serious stuff, then you also avoid a lot of drama and pain. Real life doesn't guarantee happy endings, and I'm okay with that. It works for me to live in the excitement of every moment. One thing I know, heroines take chances, and that has become my life's motto.

OUR FIRST FULL DAY HAS BEEN JAM-PACKED FULL OF BACK-TO-BACK panels. Quinn has this entire week scheduled to the minute. She's determined to grasp every bit of wisdom she can, using it to learn about publishing and business. Me, I'm in love with things like model ice cream social and hot dude bingo.

They have set aside the evenings for mixers and fun casual activities. And I'm looking forward to tonight's festivities of Cocktails and Authors. Two of my favorite things. I get to drink and I meet cool people. As we enter the busy ballroom, I scan the room. It's full of faces that are quickly becoming familiar. We're all following similar schedules and it is easy to make new friends in a crowd like this. We already have so much in common. It's like summer camp for book nerds.

"Let's get a drink," I suggest, weaving through the tiny groups of people huddled at tables and surrounding an empty makeshift dance floor. Quinn follows me over to the bar and we each order a white wine. Sipping on our drinks, we meander through the people, stopping to talk to people as we go. The crowd is getting fuller and I'm guessing it has something to do with the mini meet n greet they have going on. Some attending authors are set up around the room meeting readers, and the intimate setting is getting a pretty good turnout. I'm happy I stuffed a few books in my bag at the last minute.

A quick glance around the room shows me that Keaton

Harris' table is practically empty. Why they have that beautiful man tucked in the shadows I'll never understand. But it's the perfect chance to get my book signed.

"Hey, come with me, Quinny. I want to get my booked signed." I grab her arm and drag her with me towards the other side of the room where the cocky author is sitting all alone and looking bored to tears.

"Oh no. I don't want to go over there, "Quinn protests. She plants her feet on the floor and I pull her like a dog towards a bath. I throw her my best exasperated look, followed by the head tilt that says, get over it *and keep walking.* I hear her groan, but ignore her. "You aren't going to ask him to touch his abs are you? I won't have any part of that," she warns. I can't help but laugh at her anxiety. I really embarrassed her at the panel earlier. She will never forgive me for that. It shouldn't amuse me as much as it does, but she's so shy sometimes that it's fun to get her riled up. Granted, I did ask him if he got turned on writing sex scenes, so maybe I took it a little too far, but he wasn't phased by it. The man is arrogant as hell. He likes the attention.

"I promise to be on my best behavior," I say to ease her worry.

"He's such a pompous ass, I don't even know why you want to talk to him," she grumbles under her breath.

"Because he's a kick ass author. I'm not asking you to sit down with him and solve the world's problems. I just want him to sign my book and look at the pretty," I say.

She huffs as we close in on the table, but I pretend not to hear her. Reputation or not, the man was insanely good looking. I wasn't going to miss my chance to see him up close. Besides, I really do like his books. He's a great writer.

As we step up to the table, Keaton sits up straighter, happy to give us his attention. "Hi," I smile sweetly as I dig in my bag for a copy of his book. "I was hoping I'd catch you. I wanted to see if you could sign a book for me."

He smiles back, the perfect panty dropper grin that gets all the ladies hot and bothered. The man has skills. "Of course, I'd be happy to. I didn't catch your name earlier during the Q&A," he says. He glances from me to Quinn and I want to kick her because she is blatantly ignoring him, looking anywhere but at him.

"I'm Lily," I say, offering my hand. He turns to Quinn, forcing her to break out of her icebox and look at him when he asks her for her name.

"I'm Quinn," she says as she fidgets under his gaze.

"Quinn," he says, repeating her name. He's staring at her, and she's not paying a lick of attention to him. I want to nudge her, but it would be too obvious. I know she thinks he's a jerk, but the man is sex on a stick and he's looking at her like she's a tall glass of water and he's just spent all day walking through the desert.

Keaton clears his throat and pulls his gaze away from my friend. "So, are you ladies here for the entire week?" He grabs the marker and opens the book I've given him.

Since Quinn is obviously not going to answer him, I do. "Uh huh, we are having the best time. We want to get out and explore the city some, but there's so much to do here that we haven't had a chance yet. This is our first time to one of these, so it's pretty exciting."

He gives me a smile and then turns to Quinn. "And you're having a good time too, Quinn?"

"It's been fun," she offers. I roll my eyes. She's not giving anything up. I almost feel bad for the guy. I'm sure he's not used to this kind of reaction.

"Do you have a book you want me to sign?" he asks her, not giving up.

Quinn says something back, but I don't hear what it is, because right then I see him. Tall, dark and handsome is at the edge of the ballroom and I am not about to lose my shot again.

"Oh, there's that Miles guy. I'll be right back, Quinny."

I probably shouldn't have ditched Quinn at Keaton Harris' table. Sometimes I don't think. I just do. She's going to be pissed, but hopefully, she'll get over it. I've been trying to track down this guy all day. I swear he can disappear faster than an audience at a David Copperfield show. I weave my way through the crowd, looking for the man in question. I only caught a glimpse of him, tall above the crowd, but it was enough to recognize his shaggy hair.

I need an up close and personal look.

I make it to the doors of the ballroom and look out, but he's not there.

"Hey, Lily." I spin when I hear my name and walk back into the darkened room. Smiling, I join the group of girls that Quinn and I met earlier in the day.

"Hey," I greet them, while sneaking a peek over my shoulder to see if I can find Dark and Handsome.

"I love your dress," one of the girls, I think her name is Lena, says.

"Thanks," I smile.

"Are you looking for someone?" her friend asks.

"Am I that obvious?" I laugh. "I saw this really hot guy I scoped out earlier. I was trying to track him down."

"Was he a model?" Lena asks, taking an interest.

"I don't think so. Maybe." He was definitely nice to look at, but he didn't strike me as the model type. "He was intriguing."

"I went to cover model bingo. I didn't even punch my card because I was too busy drooling," Lena says. "I have no shame about that."

I laugh, liking this girl more and more. "I saw them all

hanging down by the bar earlier, maybe you should get thirsty," I suggest.

"I am feeling pretty parched," she says, feigning a cough.

We're all laughing and encouraging her when my bestie joins the group and grabs a hold of my arm in desperation.

"I'm ready to go," Quinn says.

"What? Already? We just got here," I point out. She crosses her arms across her chest and gives me a hard look. Yeah, I'm in trouble.

"Look, you don't have to come with me, but I'm tired and I just want to go to bed."

I consider it for a moment, letting her go back to the room alone. I know her well enough to know that sometimes she just needs some space to get over things. But I feel bad for having left her back at the table, and so I agree to go with her. Maybe after she calms down, she'll want to come back downstairs.

We say quick goodbyes to our new friends and then I follow her out of the ballroom.

We walk in silence as we move to the bank of elevators. The quiet kills me. I search for something to say that will ease the tension, but nothing comes. So instead I say, "Man, these shoes are killing me. I should never wear new heels to a party. I know better." I wait for her to agree, to tell me I will never learn, but she says nothing.

When she refuses to speak in the elevator, I continue to rattle on with pointless facts, determined to get her to crack. She ignores me, not interested at all. This is the silent treatment. I ignore it and continue my chatter as we make our way to the room.

"Okay, I'm sorry," I finally say as she closes the door behind us.

"Sorry? You left me to the wolves, Lil. To run off after some guy that you never even tracked down. You left me standing there with Keaton Harris and I was a complete idiot. It was mortifying," she groans, clearly irritated with my signature flightiness.

"I'm sure it wasn't that bad," I point out, taking a seat at the foot of the bed as she paces the room in front of me.

"Oh, it was indeed *that bad*." Quinn flops down beside me, exasperated.

"Tell me what happened," I urge. Her face is all contorted at the memory and I feel bad for having left her there. Not that Quinn can't hold her own with someone like Keaton Harris, but I know she didn't even want to go to his table in the first place.

"I basically told him I wasn't a groupie, and I wasn't going to sleep with him," she says. I take a second to close my mouth, because she's shocked me still with it gaping open.

"He asked you to sleep with him?" I ask, shocked. I probably shouldn't be, knowing his reputation, but I only left her alone for a minute.

"No. That's the crazy part. I just blurted it out like he'd handed me his room key. It was horrible, Lil."

"What did he say?" I ask cautiously.

"He laughed. If I never see him again, it will be too soon. I can't believe I did that. Just being around him puts me on edge. If we see him around we're running the other direction," she huffs.

Poor Quinn. She's not one to jump into uncomfortable situations. She always jokes that I like to throw her into them. It's no wonder she's mad at me.

"I'm sorry," I offer, hoping she can hear the sincerity in my voice.

"It was just so embarrassing," she admits. I can feel her fire starting to fade and I hope that it means that she'll forgive me pretty fast.

"Well, look at this way, Quinny, you put him in his place. Good for you."

She laughs, humoring me.

"Seriously. It sounds like you held your own. I'm sorry I left you. I won't do it again," I say.

She rolls her eyes, "Right."

"Hey!" She laughs at me and her shoulders relax a little. I know I've been forgiven. Lucky for me, Quinn has a lot of patience with me. It's a good thing, because I seem to be pretty good at testing it.

"So what do you want to do now? We can go grab a late dinner and see a little bit of the city," I suggest.

Quinn shakes her head. "I think I just want to read a little and go to sleep. I want to forget this entire night happened."

That Keaton guy did a number on her tonight. I can see her resolve to hide out, at least for now.

"Okay," I say reluctantly. It's still early, but I won't push her. Not this time. She needs to lick her wounds for a bit. "I'm going to change out of this dress then." I pat her leg and move across the room to the suitcase that lies beneath the pile of clothes I tried and discarded in my rush to get ready earlier. Grabbing a pair of jeans and my favorite worn Royals Baseball sweatshirt, I head to the bathroom and pull my hair back into a ponytail, the long waves thick as they hang down my back. I'm still wired and not ready to settle. I'm kicking myself for leaving her earlier. I hate that I put her in a position that upset her enough to shut down for the entire night.

I walk back out, ready to apologize again and try to change her mind to go out, just the two of us, maybe walk around, but she's already in her pajamas and beneath the covers, a book open in her lap.

"I really am sorry, Quinny," I say.

She shrugs. "It's fine. I'm just tired. You don't have to stay here with me," she says.

"No, it's cool. We can buddy read," I offer. She smiles, shows me the cover of her book. I grab my copy from the table and plop down on the mattress beside her. We sit in silence as we both begin to read content in the company, just like we always have been. Lost in the world of fairytales while grounding each other to reality.

It's only an hour or so later when I look up and see that Quinn has fallen asleep, the book on her chest. A quick glance at the clock tells me it's only nine-thirty. I consider reading more, but the truth is I'm still antsy. Getting up, I take the book from her and take her glasses off and set them on the night-stand. She opens her eyes, groggy and disoriented.

"Sleep. I'm going to run downstairs and wander a bit. I'll be back soon." She nods at me and turns to her side, pulling the pillow to her and making her own private cocoon.

I slip on my shoes, grab my room key, wallet, my phone and a stack of books, including the one I've been reading and slip out into the hallway. There are a few people milling about and I smile and chat with a couple as I wait for the elevator. I have no idea where I'm going, but I'm not one who needs a destination. The bar downstairs is loud with people lingering. Constant laughter fills the open space, echoing off of the walls and turning the volume up. Normally, I'd jump right into a scene like that, but tonight I just kind of want to to find a place to chill. A quick stop at the front desk leads me out onto the busy street with the promise of an all-night diner with the best pie and coffee around.

The air is brisk as I cross the street and find the restaurant with its classic red vinyl booths and checkered floor. It's busy, but I spot an empty table in the back and the hostess is happy to let me sit there. I set my stack of books beside me and order a piece of apple pie and a coffee before taking in my surroundings. This is my kind of place and I take a moment to soak in the atmosphere. I'm tempted to forgo the books I brought and just people watch, but escape wins out as the waitress brings me my order. I thank her with a smile and after pouring an obscene amount of sugar into my cup; I pull a book from the top of the stack and settle in, pulling my legs beneath me. It only takes a few pages before the noise and activity of the diner completely fades away and I'm lost in the story, quickly falling in love with another fictional version of the man of my dreams. In fact, I'm so engrossed in the book I don't even notice the tall dark stranger that has stopped beside my booth. Which is a shame, because he happens to be the very man who has been distracting me all day.

"Hi." The voice that interrupts me is deep and commands my attention. I lift my eyes, smiling when I see Dark and Handsome standing at my table. You see? You put shit in the universe and she delivers it right to you.

I swallow the instant smile the sight of him begs for.

"Hi," I reply, giving him nothing more. I take him in, appreciating the view up close. I'm staring, but I don't care. He's worth staring at. And I've been wanting this up close and personal look all day long. It does not disappoint.

"Are you waiting for someone or can I join you?" he asks. He's not nervous at all. I like his confidence.

"Depends. Are you a serial killer?"

"I'm not."

"A stage five clinger that can't take no for an answer?" I ask.

He smiles, "Nope."

I pretend to think about his answers and then ask one final question. "Do you live with your mom?"

He laughs, "Not since I was seventeen."

"Sit," I offer. He slides into the booth, his smile warm and genuine. "Do you have a name?" I ask.

"Miles. You?"

"Lily," I smile. I try to rein it in, but I can't resist the pull. He's only spoken a few words and I'm already craving more of them.

"It's nice to finally meet you, Lily," he says, leaning back against the red vinyl booth.

"Finally?" I ask, my eyebrow raised with suspicion.

"I saw you earlier. At one of the panels across the street," he admits.

"You were at a romance convention?" I laugh, even though I already know this. But teasing him is fun.

His eyes crinkle with his amusement. "I was working."

"Filling water glasses?" I ask, trying to hide my smile. Shit. He's gorgeous.

"Something like that," he says with a low chuckle.

"But you aren't working now?" I ask, stirring the coffee in front of me.

"I have weird hours," he explains vaguely.

"Lucky me," I flirt.

"So, what are you reading?" he asks, nodding to the stack of paperbacks beside me. I hold up the one I started before he showed up and show him the cover.

"It's a love story," I smile.

"You like happy endings then?" he asks.

"I don't like endings," I reply with a shrug.

His gaze captures mine and I have to fight not to look away from the intensity behind his eyes.

He's still in the suit he was wearing earlier. It's sexy. I wouldn't mind wearing that white shirt sometime. He clears his throat and I realize that I'm staring at him again, undressing him with my mind. I'd feel bad, but let's face it, guys do it all the time. Why shouldn't we get in on the fun?

"Nice suit," I say, just so he can see the direction of my thoughts.

"Nice sweatshirt," he smiles back. I glance down at the Kansas City Royals sweatshirt I am wearing.

"Do you like baseball?" I ask.

"Sure," he replies.

I like the way he lets me ask my random questions, playing along like he's known me forever.

"What team?"

He grins, "Yankees." I make a face and he laughs.

"It's my home team. Don't hate," he says. His good-natured smile has me smiling back, despite his poor taste in sports teams. I like the way he relaxes against his seat, comfortable.

"You're from New York." It's not a question, but somehow his admission surprises me.

"Ever been?" he asks.

I make another face and shake my head. "Not my scene," I admit. This makes him scoff, like he can't believe the absurdity of my words. I felt the same way when he talked about the Yankees.

"Where are you from?" he asks, as if my answer will explain my dislike of the big city.

I laugh, "Missouri." I point to my shirt. "Home team."

His chuckle rumbles deep in his chest, the vibration forcing it to the surface.

"Can't say I've ever been there," he smiles.

"It's nice. We have great BBQ," I huff, pretending to look annoyed at his dismissal of my home state.

"I like BBQ," he says, and his smile wins me over. He pulls me in like a magnet, his charisma like a beacon calling me home.

"New York BBQ?" I ask with a raised eyebrow, like there is such a thing.

"I travel a lot," he smirks. Did he just wink at me?

"Lots of romance conventions?" I smile, teasing him.

"A few," he admits as the waitress comes to check on us. Miles orders a coffee and then asks me how the pie is. I glance down, realizing that I was so engrossed in my book I'd forgotten to eat it.

"Pie is amazing," I smile, and he orders some of his own.

"So, you're here for the entire week?" he asks once the waitress leaves.

"Yes. I'm here with my best friend."

"Lucky me," he says casually.

"Lucky you?" I ask, wondering if he's one of those creepy guys who goes straight for the threesome suggestion. That would be a shame. He's so pretty.

"Lucky that I have all week to win you over," he clarifies.

"You seem pretty confidant," I say, trying to keep my face neutral and keep the upper hand in this little Tete d' Tete. But it's like my lips can't help themselves. The goofy grin is like an involuntary reaction to his voice. When he smiles, I practically melt.

"I'd go with hopeful," he replies as the waitress brings his pie and coffee. I smile across the table at him, feeling myself slipping under his charm and not really caring. After all, I'd been chasing him around the hotel all day. Now that he's sitting across from me, I'm certain the chase was worth it... even if it was he who finally found me.

"This pie really is amazing," he says. I pull my eyes from his and pick up my fork, knowing the sugar high will have nothing on the high I'm getting from this guy.

Two hours later, I feel like I've known Miles for years. It's not like we talked about anything of importance. We simply drifted from subject to subject with the easy cadence of old friends enjoying each other's company. He's funny, making me laugh so hard my stomach hurts, but he also smart and willing to jump into a heated discussion about politics and aliens. Don't ask me how one led to the other because I'm not sure how we made the leap because we didn't mention Roswell once and it was still effortless. It's rare that I feel this kind of connection with a person so easily, but he intrigues me and I want to hear more and more. I would be perfectly happy sitting here with him until the sun colors the horizon. But when I yawn so big that my eyes water, he suggests we head back to the hotel and get some rest.

I'm disappointed, but so exhausted that I can't really argue with him. He pays for our pie and coffee and then takes my stack of books in his arms and leads me out of the diner. Now that he's standing beside me I can appreciate just how tall he is. I feel tiny standing beside him. He practically looms over me and it makes me long to feel what his arms would feel like wrapped around me. I could get lost in an embrace like his. The idea sounds heavenly.

"What floor are you on?" he asks, pulling me from my thoughts.

"Six."

"Mind if I walk you to your door?" he asks. There's no hint of expectation or innuendo. Of course he knows Quinn is asleep in our room, so there's no way I'm inviting him in. Still, he could have asked me to his room. Would I have gone? What am I thinking? I met the man not even three hours ago.

We don't speak as we make our way down the hall, but there is something in the air between us. Anticipation. The urge to continue this evening through morning. I think I'd like to see his face cast in the glow of early morning sun.

"This is me," I say as we make it to my door.

"Thanks for letting me crash your evening. It made mine much more enjoyable," he says. A small smile pulls at the corner of his lips, teasing and playful, but his eyes hold a seriousness that speaks way beyond his words. The combination is heady and intoxicating.

"Maybe we'll have the chance to do it again sometime," I offer.

"I wouldn't have it any other way," he says confidently.

He makes it hard to play coy. Sometimes he even makes me feel shy. It's not something that I'm used to, and I'm still trying to decide if I like it.

"Goodnight, Miles," I smile. I turn towards the door, but he reaches for me and before I can catch my breath, my back is against the wall and his handsome face is only a breath from mine.

I wait for him to kiss me. I breathe him in as my heart rushes with anticipation. But he doesn't kiss me. Not like I want him to. Instead of giving me what I want, he brushes his lips against my own with feather soft strokes, barely giving me a taste of all he is capable of. When he pulls back, I feel the space instantly and fight the urge to pull him back to me. Normally, I would do just that, take what I want. Enjoy everything the moment has to offer. But with Miles, I like the waiting. I like wondering what the next day might bring. "Goodnight, Lily."

He steps back, that hint of a smile playing at his lips. I'm starting to think it's his default setting. I work to catch my breath and watch as he saunters back down the hall and around the corner. Once he's out of sight I sneak inside, closing the door and leaning back against it. The swoon clings to me, enveloping me in a fog.

Quinn is sleeping and while I know I shouldn't wake her up, I'm dying to tell her about meeting Miles. I doubt that she'd be thrilled if I woke up her up, especially after the night she's had. And since I'd had a hand in the bad turn it had taken, I figure it will be better to hold on to my story until morning. I can push Quinn, but even I know she has limits.

Instead, I float around the room, high on my Miles encounter, as I change into my sleep shorts and get ready for bed. Climbing under the covers, I stare at Quinn, willing her to wake up on her own so I can talk to her, but she is dead to the world. With a sigh, I open the book I was reading when Miles had showed up at my table. I stare at the words, but nothing is sinking in. So, I replay our conversation over and over instead until I finally drift off to sleep.

I haven't stopped thinking about Lily since I left her at her door. I'm kicking myself for not getting her number because now I have to find her in this sea of people. I can do it, but it might take me longer, especially since I'm working. Lord knows my brother isn't going to let me wander off to look for a girl when I'm supposed to be attending to his every whim.

Running into her at the diner was dumb luck. I just wanted to get out of the hotel for a bit and there she was. The girl from the panel, the one with the sassy comment and the tight little body I'd been thinking about ever since. She looked so adorable all wrapped up in her oversized sweatshirt, messy hair, all engrossed in a book that I just stopped and watched her for a bit before I went over to her table. She had an entire stack of books with her, like she was going to stay and read them all.

I smile at the memory as I make my way towards the first meeting room of the day, coffee in hand. My eyes dart back and forth, searching for her dark hair, eager to find her and make plans to see her again. I want to keep talking to her. I want to give her that kiss I teased her with last night. I want to spend as much time with Lily, getting to know as much as I can about her. And that starts with finding her.

It doesn't take long. The fates are smiling down on me again when I spot her at the other end of a long corridor. My heartbeat picks up and I nearly toss my coffee to the floor in a rush to catch up with her.

"Lily- wait up," I call out, jogging to catch up. She spins towards me and welcomes me with a smile that could knock me straight to my knees. I take a moment to find my breath and my words. "I was hoping I'd run into you."

She laughs, "You nearly did." She stands easily, her slight frame commanding every bit of my attention. She's stunning, even casually dressed in a pair of faded jeans, and a red sweater with the word *Nope* written across it.

"Have dinner with me tonight," I say quickly. Her smile widens and her head tilts ever so slightly as she studies me.

"You want to take me to dinner?" she asks, as if I wasn't perfectly clear in my request.

"That's what I said." Her eyes dance with amusement as I wait for her answer.

"I can't," she says simply. I'm sure my face falls along with my heart. Straight to the floor. I wasn't expecting that. "I can't ditch my friend. This is our girl's trip. She'd kill me if I left her to have dinner with some handsome stranger I'd met at the diner across the street."

Handsome stranger. I smile.

Okay. I can work with this.

"I see. But if you could, would you want to have dinner with the handsome stranger that you met at the diner across the street?"

She smiles, "If I could? Of course, I would. He's the best stranger I've met on this trip."

I smirk. I can't help myself.

"So, bring her along," I suggest.

Lily laughs, her head falling back with the sound. Fuck, this girl is beautiful. "Obviously, you haven't met Quinn. I don't think she's much on being the third wheel. Or part of some kinky threesome, if that's what you had in mind."

It's my turn to laugh, "No? Shit, there goes my night." She shrugs in mock apology. "Listen, what if we make it a casual dinner? You bring your friend and I'll bring my brother," I offer.

Her brows furrow. "Your brother? Are you having your family reunion at the book convention?" she teases.

"I'm here with my brother. He's a writer. I help him out at things like this," I say. I rarely drop my brother's name, nor do I invite him on dates, but this could be my only option. Plus, I think he likes Quinn. He mentioned her last night, so I doubt he'll mind.

"Your brother is a writer?" she asks, almost as if she doesn't believe me.

"Keaton Harris," I admit, reluctantly. Her eyes go wide and I worry that maybe I've ruined everything by telling her. But she laughs like I'm hilarious. "What?" I ask, feeling a familiar annoyance settle in. If she asks me to introduce her so, she can hook up with him I will lose my shit.

"Nothing. I mean, now that you mention it, I guess I can see the resemblance." I scowl at her words and she reaches out and brushes my arm with her fingers. "You're way hotter," she says. I laugh, the tension leaving my body. This is what pulls me to her. Her effortless charm and zero give a fuck attitude. It's her confidence and the way she carries herself. No apologies.

"I'm laughing because if I tell Quinn that she has to have dinner with Keaton Harris, she will throttle me."

"Then don't tell her," I say.

She thinks on it for a moment before saying, "Just show up and offer her up to the wolves? That's evil. She's my best friend."

"His bark is worse than his bite," I say.

"But hers isn't," she says.

"Might be good for him," I offer.

After another pause, Lily nods her head in agreement. "It might be good for her too. How about we meet you at eight?"

Lily

Maybe it's wrong to drag Quinn to a dinner where I know her current arch nemesis is joining us, but I choose to ignore that tiny fact. I mean, the truth is the girl needs to get out and face some of her fears once in a while. It's up to me to make sure that happens. Besides, it's dinner. It's safe. It will be good for her.

Yeah, she's going to kill me. She's already complained the entire walk here, and she thinks it's just some random guy. My plan is to play dumb and not let her know that I knew Miles' brother was actually Keaton Harris. We'll pretend it is a surprise for both of us.

I'm a horrible friend.

Or the best friend ever.

We'll see how the night goes.

Quinn follows me into the restaurant and as I approach the hostess, I hear a familiar voice call out, "Lily! You made it." I turn to see Miles. My heart surging unexpectedly as he leans in to kiss my cheek.

"Hi," I say, my voice quiet as I try to catch my breath. He smiles and turns his attention to Quinn to introduce himself.

"You must be Quinn," he smiles, offering his hand. She takes it with a weak smile that barely covers the look of horror on her face. She must have spotted Keaton, who is quickly approaching our circle.

I conveniently become engrossed in my surroundings as Miles introduces her to his brother. Honestly, I'm a little afraid to look at her. It's possible her death glare will send me to the ground in an instant.

"Shall we get a table?" I ask cheerfully, as if nothing in the world is amiss. The sharp elbow in my side tells me she's not letting me off the hook so easily. I give her my best innocent smile. She's not buying it, but I know she'll forgive me, eventually.

We slide into a large booth and settle in. I like how even though the booth is big enough for us to spread out, Miles sits close enough that I can feel the heat of his body beside me. His leg brushes against mine and I feel the flush through my entire body. It makes me want more. It's attraction, infatuation, but something more I can't quite put my finger on. I want to peel away all of his layers and examine each and every one. I want to stare at him in silence and appreciate the shape of every line that makes up his perfect face. I want to listen to the way his breath falls and changes with his mood. I'm fascinated with him. He's a complete stranger, and yet I already feel like I've known him for years. He's a mystery that needs unraveled and I won't settle until I figure it out, put all the pieces together where they belong and then thoroughly enjoy them.

"I'm glad you tricked her and meet us for dinner," Miles says low in my ear. We glance over to the other couple at the other end of the booth. I briefly wonder if I should remove all the knives from the table, just in case Keaton keeps pushing my best friend's buttons. She looks both flushed and murderous right now.

"Let's wait and see if we survive it," I whisper back.

"Even if we don't, it will be worth it," he says. His breath is hot against my skin and suddenly I don't care if they are getting along or not. One glance up at Miles' handsome face looking down at me and I'm completely enraptured.

Kiss me. I'm begging him, but he only smiles, still refusing to give me what I want. Sure, we're in a restaurant, but I don't care. I'm dying to taste his lips. They look soft, but I know they are powerful enough to leave me breathless, to leave me swollen and begging for more.

I hear a feel a soft groan against his chest as he stares down at me. It's like we've just had an entire conversation in the space of a moment. Made promises, set expectations, all without saying a word. I give him a small smile, letting him know he's not getting away without giving me what I want tonight. I only have him for a few days and I don't plan on wasting any of it.

The night has gone way better than I could have hoped for. Not only am I pretty sure that Quinn isn't going to kill me for throwing her into the lion's den, but I'm thinking she is actually having a good time. So much so, that when Miles and I leave them alone to wander to the carousel, I don't worry about her at all. I know my best friend well enough to know she would have put a stop to it had she had any sense of discomfort. Quinn is not afraid to say no when she means it. It's a good thing, because I've asked a lot of her over the years.

"I haven't been on one of these since I was a kid," Miles laughs, sitting upright on one of the brightly colored ponies as we go round and round among flashing lights and organ music. The salty breeze coming off the bay tickles my nose as I grip the pole and lean way back in my saddle. I hear Miles' deep rumble of a laugh and I snap the memory up to keep for later.

I throw him a big smile, "You have really been missing out,"

"Obviously," he says with a flirty wink, one that hits me square in the heart and has me looking for more.

"Do you dance, Miles Harris?" I ask him on a whim. His eyebrows raise along with the corner of his mouth. He has the same sexy smirk as his brother, only his has me wanting to kiss it right off of his face.

"If I have the right partner," he teases.

"Good, I know just the place," I smile, hopping down from my horse as the ride comes to a stop. I take his hand as we exit with all the kids. Grabbing my phone, I shoot off a text to Quinn to let her know what our plans are so we can meet up. She takes a few minutes, but declines saying she's tired. I ask her if she's okay with Keaton and she assures me he's not as bad as she thought, and they've had a nice talk.

Reassured that Keaton will walk her back, I turn to my own Harris brother. "Looks like it's just us," I smile, tucking my phone into my pocket.

"Still want to go dancing?" he asks.

"Hell, yeah I do," I say, eager to spend more time with him. He offers me his hand, and I let him lead me down the street.

An hour and a half later, we're tucked away in a dark corner of the club. My skin is damp from my exertion on the dance floor and tiny goosebumps break across my skin as I begin to cool, my heart settling back to normal rhythms. I take a moment to admire my date for the evening as the waitress drops off our drinks. His hair sticks to his forehead, sweat glistening around his temples. I imagine running my fingers through it, messing it up. Tugging at it as he holds himself above me, his exertion not from dancing but from taking my body for his own.

He must see the thought drift across my eyes, because he gives me a seductive smile, his honey brown eyes darkening a shade as he runs his thumb across the scruff along his jaw. I let that fantasy play out too. That scruff, my thighs.

I'm not shy about letting him know how attracted I am to him. I've wanted him since the moment I saw him in the hallway yesterday. He hasn't even kissed me yet, but I've had him a hundred different ways in my mind.

"You're the best part of my trip so far," I admit quietly. I'm not sure if he even hears me over the noise, but the words feel good on my lips. I lean towards him, needing to be closer to him, to remove the space between us.

"Same," he says, his eyes holding mine, the space between us shrinking with every breath. I'm so ready for him to kiss me. I can feel his breath against my lips, a whisper away, and I trace my tongue across them in anticipation. My eyes flutter closed, waiting for the soft feel of his mouth against my own. But when it doesn't happen, I open them to see him staring at me, still close, still intense.

"You didn't kiss me," I say, stating the obvious, mostly to make sure he knows that I wanted him to.

"Not yet," he says, leaning back and sipping his drink. And somehow the promise of the kiss is just as sexy as if he'd done it.

Normally, I would take what I want. But with him, the anticipation is nearly as good. I smile at him and sit back, giving him the point. My heart beating a little faster than normal, my stomach twisting in the most delicious way.

The man is good.

I take a minute and another two sips of my drink to stop thinking about his almost kiss before attempting normal conversation. He doesn't break the silence, letting me sit there with the anticipation, making friends, like he's setting his trap. Doesn't he know I'd go willingly?

It's fine, I'll wait. It gives me time to unravel the man. Lucky for me, getting to know him is just as thrilling for me. "Okay, so I get to ask you questions then," I say.

He smiles. God, it's devastating. Like a freaking Disney prince. He smiles and I can't help but smile back. It's automatic. He takes away all of my cool and I don't even care.

"Ask away," he says.

"Should we start easy and work up to the hard stuff?" I ask.

"Your call. I'm not afraid of anything you throw at me," he shrugs.

"Sounds like a dare," I say.

"Oh, Lily, I shouldn't admit this so soon, but I'm already at your mercy," he says.

I huff, "Says the boy who won't even kiss me."

He leans in towards me, his voice low and sultry as he says, "Only because I'm not sure I'll stop with just a kiss." He holds my gaze, letting his words settle like a promise, burn like fire deep in my core, and I want to crawl over the table and straddle him. Then he lets loose that devilish smirk and sits back, sipping his drink like nothing happened.

"Sounds tempting." I say. I'm not afraid of him or anything he might have planned for me.

He holds my gaze for a long moment, both of us lost in our own vision of what how it will play out. I say will, because we both know it will go down at some point. There's no way we're walking away without satisfying this growing craving.

"You haven't asked a question yet," he says finally, clearing his throat.

"Okay, we'll start with the normal stuff. Career. You work with your brother now. Do you love it? Is it your forever job?" I ask him.

Miles thinks for a moment and then shrugs. "I don't know that it's my forever job. I love the work. I love hanging out with my best friend and the travel. I don't have too many responsibilities tying me down, and it provides me a lot of opportunities. But to be honest, I don't really know what my big forever dream job is. If this is it, or if it's something else. Is that bad?"

Smiling, I shake my head. I knew I liked him.

"Not at all. I think most people jump into a career choice because it's expected of them. I mean, why should we know at 17 or 18 what we want to do for the rest of our lives? Most of the time we don't even know who we are yet. Hell, I'm twenty-two and I barely have a grasp on it. I think we'd all be a lot happier if we just let it find us instead of forcing something to make our parents or society happy. Life is short, do things that make you happy. Live the life you're given and don't settle for what people expect of you, ya know?"

He smiles, his eyes warm as he takes me in. "I agree. What about you? You said the other night that you do event planning. Does that make you happy? Is it your forever job?" he asks.

"I think so. I feel like I'm one of the lucky ones. I love my job. I mean, I might change my mind at some point, but for now it makes me happy. I enjoy going to work and there are lots of people who can't say that."

"So, tell me about it. What type of events do you plan?" he asks, and for some reason I believe he's actually interested in my answer. And so, I tell him. I rattle on and he listens, intently. Our structured question time quickly turning into an easy conversation that flows seamlessly back and forth.

Aside from Quinn, I don't know that I've ever been able to talk this comfortably with someone. I mean, I can talk to a wall post, but not about things that are important. Not without wondering if I'm sharing too much or if I'm giving too much of myself away. With Miles I just want to keep digging and when he digs back, I want to answer.

And God, he makes me smile and laugh and I don't know how it happens, but the lights are flashing, and the club is closing down and we're being forced out of our little bubble and back onto the street like no time has passed at all. And once again, I feel like I don't want the night to end.

We start back towards the hotel, our walk slow, like two kids dragging their feet, refusing to give up their fun. Miles slips his hand into mine; he doesn't look to me to see if it's okay, he just knows that it is. I glance down at our entwined fingers, loving how they fit together and the way his thumb runs lazy circles across my skin. It sends a shot of adrenaline through me, leaving me feeling needy and intoxicated. More than the whiskey I've sipped on all night.

"What are you doing tomorrow?" Miles asks as we make our way along the darkened streets.

"Same thing I did today. Book things," I say.

"Me too," he responds.

"Want to do something after book things?" he asks.

"I'm supposed to go to the piano bar with some friends. Want to meet me there?" I ask.

"Are you going to sing on the piano?" he asks.

"I might."

"Then, I wouldn't dare miss it."

His hand, still in mine, he pulls me to a sudden stop. I glance over at him, questioning, but he just tugs at me to follow him. Of course, I follow him and soon he has me tucked in a quiet alley just off of the sidewalk. I give him a sly smile as he slowly maneuvers us until my back finds the brick wall of one building, his arms caging me in. I stare up at him as he looks down at me with that same hungry expression that he had earlier. This time he'd better deliver.

"Need something?" I ask.

He nods, "Desperately."

His face, so close to mine that I can see the swirls of color in his eyes. I can see the tiny freckle that sits just beside his nose and the way his lips form the perfect pout without even trying. He holds my gaze, pulling me closer with that look alone.

"Don't leave me waiting this time, Harris," I tell him.

His hand finds my face, his fingertips stroking across my cheek with feather softness, drifting down the curve of my throat and around the back of my neck where he gives me a gentle, yet possessive squeeze.

"Fuck, you are something else," he says, his voice deep and wanting. The passion there, for a kiss leaves my entire body trembling. My gut twists and I feel like I will die if he doesn't close the space between us. I feel like this is my first kiss, the only kiss that has ever mattered. I need it like I need my next breath.

He pulls me to him, his mouth brushing across mine, softly, teasing, tentative. It's like maybe he really doesn't trust himself to kiss me. Like maybe he really is worried that he won't stop and we'll desecrate this alley in the most delicious way. I'm not completely against it.

But then, just when I'm sure he's going to pull away he pushes into me, the weight of him against my body, his hands on either side of my face as his mouth comes down hard on mine, devouring me like I am what gives him oxygen to live.

I whimper and as my lips part his tongue finds mine, and the kiss goes to a place where my rational thought no longer has a pass. My hands are everywhere, trying to cling to him, yet touch every part of his body. I'm pretty sure I'm trying to climb him like a tree. So, when he lifts me, pressing me harder against the wall, his hard body, and his impressive erection in all the right places, I want to sing with happiness.

Holy shit, I don't want him to ever break away from me.

He's murmuring words against my lips, against my neck, my collarbone, and he grinds against me as he does. I can barely catch my breath and yet I don't want him to stop. I don't need oxygen. It is totally overrated.

"Lily," he groans.

"Don't stop kissing me," I tell him.

I feel his smile against my neck, and unfortunately my plea actually causes him to slow down. His kisses become less frenzied, more languid, and I'm pretty sure I let out a little cry.

"Fuck, I told you. I told you I would have a hard time just kissing you," he says.

"I told you not to stop," I huff.

He pulls back, his forehead resting against mine as we both try to catch our breath. He still holding me, my legs wrapped around him, his cock pressed against me in the most delicious way.

"I can't very well fuck you in this alley. As much as I want to, I'd hate myself for it." He kisses my nose and I swear my heart melts at the simple gesture.

"It would suck if we got arrested," I agree.

He laughs. "They probably wouldn't put us in the same cell."

I sigh, "Fine. We'll have to continue this at another time then." He kisses me once more, this time holding back and keeping it soft and sweet. Then he slowly lowers me back to the ground. My legs feel wobbly and he has to hold me up until I regain my balance.

"You okay?" he asks, his cocky grin firmly in place.

"You're pretty proud of yourself, aren't you?" I tease.

"I mean, I could be happier," he admits, offering me his hand. I take it and we continue our walk back to the hotel like we didn't just turn our entire world upside down.

Holy shit, I am in so much trouble with this guy.

I step into the tiny bar and take a second to adjust to the sheer volume of banging piano keys and a mass of people singing along to "Living on a Prayer" like their life depends on it. My eyes search the crowd, everyone tucked into booths and tiny tables like sardines. Finally, I see her in a long black booth with about ten other ladies. Looks like I'm outnumbered. Still totally worth it.

I make my way through the people, dodging martini carrying waitresses and slide into the booth beside Lily. Her eyes light up and she wraps her tiny arms around my neck. "You made it!" she says excitedly, planting a kiss to my cheek.

I have missed her. I didn't see her all day and after last night, my need for her has grown exponentially.

"Hey," I smile. Lily introduces me to everyone at the table and they all wave, welcoming me happily. Everyone except her friend, Quinn, who is too busy looking back at the door. Probably to see if I brought Keaton with me. I left my brother with his laptop. I should probably tell him that Quinn is here, but he told me not to disturb him when he was writing. He said he had to get shit done because he had plans tomorrow.

The music shifts into an old Cheap Trick song and the waitress comes over to take my drink order. I order a whiskey and Lily shifts her body, so she's leaning into me. I can smell her shampoo and it's enough to make me drunk. I instantly want to kiss her the way I did last night. Everything about this girl makes me want to own her. Probably because I know I can't.

She's intoxicating and addicting, and I can't get enough of her. Lily sings beside me, dancing in her seat. The room is full of action and excitement, but it's hard to pull my eyes away from her. She just radiates energy. It sparks from her skin and everyone around her feeds off of it. I know I do. I feel the charge just sitting here beside her.

I know this is just a vacation fling, but I know I'll be thinking about her long after this week is over. In fact, I'm wondering if there is any way that I'll be able to get enough of her to walk away and not feel completely unsatisfied.

Probably not.

She smiles at me, big and bright, like I'm her favorite person in the entire world. Like I have colored her world with rainbows by being here beside her. Shit, how does she do that? How does she make me feel so special when I've only known her for a few days?

Each song moves to the next, the crowd getting louder with each drink. Everyone ready to belt out every cover song in the catalog, including Lily. "Hey, let me out. I want to make a request," she says, nudging me with her elbow. She holds a ten-dollar bill in her hand and waves it in the air excitedly. I slide out and watch as she shimmies her way through the crowd to the pianos. She shoves her money into the overflowing tip jar on top and writes down her song request. I watch as she winks to the man sitting behind the keys and then saunters back to me. She raises to her toes and presses a kiss to my lips before sliding back into her spot.

"What song did you pick?" I ask.

"Oh no, I'm not telling. You have to wait and see."

"Afraid you picked a song everyone will hate, and you'll be the only one singing?" I tease.

"Hardly. I picked an amazing song. One of the best, actually. But doubtful you'll know it." She sips her drink and gives me a mischievous sidelong glance.

"Sounds like a challenge?" I shoot back.

She shrugs as her lips tip up with the hint of a smile. "I guess we'll see."

It takes 5 songs before a set of familiar notes sends Lily into a fit of squeals. I'm guessing this is her song. And I can't help but laugh as she bangs the table with her palms. "YES!" She yells it out and the surrounding crowd follows suit. It's not one of the normal standards, and it's a song I haven't heard in so long that I take a minute to even place it. Honestly, if my parents hadn't been fans, I'm not sure I'd even know it. But Lily belts it out right along with the piano players.

"Air Supply? Really?" I laugh, completely surprised by her choice, but here she is belting out every word to "Making Love Out of Nothing at All" at the top of her lungs with a dramatic flair that puts anyone else in this room to shame. The girls at the table cheer her on and it just adds to her excitement. Right now, she is the star of her own show and I can't take my eyes off of her as she grabs my hand and sings to me. And when she stands up in the booth and whips her hair around, I think I might actually fall in love with her a little bit.

Maybe that's why as the ending crescendo hits I find myself standing up beside her, joining her in the freedom that comes with singing at the top of my lungs to a cheesy love song in the middle of a crowded room of strangers. Because this is what she meant about living in the moment. Without fear of judgment. She makes me want to live like that too.

The song ends and the crowd cheers as we return to our seats, laughing.

"Air Supply?" I tease.

"Best. Song. Ever," she says proudly.

. . .

IT'S LATE WHEN WE ALL FILE OUT OF THE BAR. LILY'S FACE FLUSHED with the heat of the bar and the martinis she sipped throughout the night. I love the way it paints her cheeks pink. The cool breeze blows up from the bay and I feel her shiver beside me as we wait for the rest of the group to join us on the sidewalk.

"You want my jacket?" I ask, leaning in, brushing my lips against her ear. She nods and I shrug out of my jacket and drape it across her shoulders, smiling when she tucks her chin in and sniffs it.

"Smells like you. I like it," she says. I laugh and she slides her arm through mine as we start to make our way up the street. The group breaks off into smaller groups, chatting or singing as they walk.

"I'm really glad that you came out with us tonight," she says, resting her head against me as we slow our steps, letting the group get further ahead of us.

"Me too. Well, until you started singing "Pour Some Sugar on Me" and nearly took me out with your elbow," I laugh.

"Well, maybe if you had poured your sugar on me, I wouldn't have had to get so rough with you," she teases.

I stop, and in one smooth, fluid move I have her leaned back in my arms in a perfect Hollywood pose. She smiles up at me, eyes bright and amused. "You want sugar?" I ask.

"I want everything," she says, breathless.

Oh, I want to give her everything.

I lean in and kiss her, soft and slow. I don't think I've ever wanted a woman as much as I do Lily. But it's so much more than just wanting to take her to bed. It's like she said, I want everything.

When I stand her back on her feet, she wobbles just a little and I hold her steady.

"You're pretty good at this whole sweeping a girl of her feet thing," I tell him.

"You think so?" I ask.

"Hmm," she murmurs. I slide my hand in hers, and we continue our walk towards the hotel.

The rest of the group has drifted far ahead of us and just like the night before, our steps slow the closer we get to our destination. Lily doesn't seem to mind, and I like having the time alone with her. It's late and I've caught her yawning a few times, but she doesn't complain or speed up. She seems perfectly content here with me.

I want to find any excuse to keep her out here with me. I want to watch the sunrise with her. But I can tell she's cold and tired, so I try to shut down the selfish part of me that wants to keep her talking. The part that wants to keep staring at her.

As we near the doors though, she squeezes my hand and looks at me with wide eyes, "Want to go upstairs and sit by the pool?"

I smile and glance up at the building. "It's cold," I say.

She just shrugs, "We'll probably be the only people up there." She lets the sentence hang between us suggestively, and I am not about to deny her anything at this point. "Besides, you'll figure out how to keep me warm, right?" She gives me that teasing look, the one that always comes with a dare. There is no way I'm going to say no. Not a chance. I'll go anywhere this girl asks me to.

"Lead the way," I agree. She laughs and squeezes my hand as we head inside. We beeline for the bank of elevators and her eyebrows dance at me as she hits the button for the roof.

She's right, the pool is deserted. Being this high, the breeze is even cooler, and I can see the instant gooseflesh that rises across Lily's skin. I'm not sure how anyone could ever brave this pool. Still, the lights surrounding the water are dim and the view is amazing.

"Come on," Lily pulls me closer to the water. For a minute I think she might jump in. Instead, she kicks off her shoes and sits down on the ledge, sliding her feet into the clear water. "Oh, it's really warm," she says, surprised. I'm not sure I believe her, but she doesn't look cold.

"Take off our shoes and sit down next to me, Miles," she encourages. Her smile, sweet and mischievous all at the same time.

Following her lead, I kick off my shoes and roll up my jeans to my knees. "How Do I Look?" I laugh.

"That's hot. I figured you'd just take your pants off," she teases. For a moment, I consider calling her bluff. Only, I'm pretty sure it's not a bluff at all. If it weren't so cold out, I might try to convince her to go skinny dipping with me.

"I have to make you work for it." I sit next to her and put my feet in. She was telling the truth. The pool is heated and pleasant, making me revisit that skinny-dipping idea.

"It feels nice, doesn't it?" she says, taking a deep breath and splashing her feet against the surface of the water.

"Amazing," I agree.

"I love the water," she says softly. "We have a pond, well, it's almost a lake, out by my parent's house. There's a dock and when I was growing up my mom and I used to go there and read books or just sit there and talk. I love it there. It's probably my favorite place in the world. But really, I love all water. It calms me down. Maybe because it reminds me of home," she says thoughtfully.

"That's a nice memory," I say, watching her. There is a faraway look in her eyes. And she takes a long moment to come back to me. When she does, she gives me a shy smile.

"My mom died when I was seven. I miss her a lot." My heart aches for her, I swear it cracks open right there. I open my mouth to say something, but she continues. "I don't tell many people that," she admits, her eyes holding mine.

I swallow hard, "Thank you for sharing it with me. I'm sure your mother was lovely."

"She was," Lily says with a deep breath. She looks back out across the pool and the silence falls around us. It's not awkward or uncomfortable at all. I rest my hand on hers, the wet concrete beneath our palms as we sit lost in our own thoughts.

I try to imagine a young Lily and what she went through. Compare that image to the free-spirited woman who I'm getting to know now. I know her mom would be so proud of her. To know she turned out to be so amazing, so captivating.

"We should get in," she says suddenly.

"What?" I ask, jolted out of the silence.

"We should get in. The pool is heated. Come on. It will be fun." She's already getting to her feet, taking credit for the idea I had when we first got here.

"Are you going to wear that pretty little dress in the water?" I ask, daring her to take it off.

"And ruin it? No way." I watch as she stands and then, in perfect slow motion, she grabs the hem and lifts. The corner of her mouth lifts slightly as she catches my gaze and refuses to let me break the stare even as she lifts the dress up and over her head. She lets it fall from her fingertips to the ground at her feet. I lose the fight and let my eyes fall with it, to the curves of her body. Her lace bra and tiny panties are nearly the color of her skin and I swallow hard, itching to touch her as my body instantly responds to the sight of her.

"Your turn," she smiles just before turning and diving into the water in a single fluid movement. No tiptoeing down the stairs, no worrying about getting her hair wet, she just jumps right in. There is no way I'm letting her jump in alone. By the time she resurfaces,

I've peeled off my shirt and am kicking away my jeans. Her smile is wide as she smooths her hair back, drops of water sliding across her skin; down her slender throat, over the roundness of her breasts. The woman is stunning, and I take a minute to catch my breath as I stare, dumbfounded, standing in my underwear.

"What are you waiting for?" she asks. I jump in beside her and when I surface, she's right there waiting to wrap her arms around my neck and pull me closer.

Her legs wrap around me and her mouth is on mine in an instant, hot and pliant against mine. The feel of her skin against mine is incredible. God, she feels amazing.

I can still taste the sweet alcohol on her tongue. It's fruity, a forbidden temptation, and I pull her even closer to me, searching for more, needing to feel her body pressed against mine. She moans against my lips as she moves against me. God, she fits against me so perfectly.

"You are so beautiful, Lily. So, fucking beautiful." I kiss her neck, the water leaving her skin slick.

I press her against the side of the pool, mostly to get some traction so I can devour her properly. I let my mouth travel along her collarbone and down to her cleavage before looking up and catching her eyes, asking for permission.

"Touch me, Miles," she breathes. I smile and my hand moves to her back where I unclasp her bra, freeing her heavy breasts from the lace. I drop the garment on the side of the pool and then cup her in my hands, lowering my mouth to take one of her perfect rose colored nipples into my mouth. Her moan makes my cock throb and I bite down gently before sucking a flicking the perfect peak with my tongue. I move to the other, letting my fingers work over the one I was forced to leave behind. She moves her body against mine, searching out friction against.

"You're so sexy. So, fucking perfect. I want to make you

come." I need to see her fall apart. I need to see her beautiful face as falls over the edge of ecstasy. I need to take her there.

"Please," she begs.

I cover her mouth with mine, kissing her deep and fast, letting myself take the things I've been craving for the past few days. She sets me on fire, turns me inside out. I'm crazy for her, Wild, needy and completely out of control with desire.

I slide my hand down her stomach, her soft pants against my mouth only turning me on more. It's like she can't catch her breath either and yet we keep fighting through, keep going because we can't stop. The need too great.

I move past the lace fabric of her panties and slide my fingers across her. Water is tricky, it can keep things from going smoothly, but as I slide my hand across her folds, I feel how wet she is, how needy she is for me and I groan against her throat as I nip across her skin.

"God, you're soaked, I've never wanted anyone as badly as I want you. You're fucking everything," I say.

"Miles, please," she begs. "I need you."

I slide one finger inside her warm heat, and she accepts me greedily. I slide in and out a few times and then add a second finger because I know she's ready for it. Rubbing my thumb over her swollen clit, she moves against me, whimpers of pleasure spilling from her lips. I let my fingers do what I wish my cock could do and I take in her sighs, the pout of her lips, her quick pants and the way her body tenses around my hand and then my name is falling from her lips and her nails are digging into my shoulders and she's fucking beautiful, the flush on her cheeks the most beautiful thing I've ever seen.

This girl wrecks me.

I'll never be the same.

I'm being lazy. Quinn has run off with her sexy vacation toy and I am still in my comfy sweatshirt, reading her advanced copy of End Game. I should go downstairs and sit in on something fun, but I'm still exhausted from my night out with Miles. I didn't drag myself in until morning, but man, it was worth the lack of sleep. I'm still on a high from that orgasm.

I think I might have actually had sex with him in that a pool if he hadn't been thinking rationally. I mean, we are strangers and safety and all. But shit. I wanted him so badly. Even after he worked me over with his magic fingers, I wanted him. Not to mention the poor guy was like stone in his pants. I felt bad. He'd insisted that he was cool with a cold shower and taking care of it himself for now. I offered. But he didn't want to disrespect the pool boy, which had made me laugh and like him a hundred times more than I already did.

The man was trouble. The perfect combination of sweet and sexy. Smart and scandalous.

Part of me wanted to text him right now and tell him to get his happy ass to my room so we could finish what we had started. But he had to be tired too. Besides, I'd see him later. And for the love of independent women everywhere, I did not need to spend every waking hour of my vacation with a boy.

Even though I kind of wanted to.

No, I will lounge right here, order room service, read a book and take a nap.

I pull my eyes away from my book when my phone pings with an incoming text, and I smile when I see the message previewed on my screen.

MILES: I'M AT YOUR DOOR.

My smile grows wider as I scramble to my feet and race to the mirror to check my appearance. My hair is pulled up in a messy bun, my sweatshirt might have a chocolate stain from the Snickers I ate for breakfast and I could certainly use some mascara, but I don't have time to worry with any of that. I grab the handle, swinging it open and take in the tall drink of water leaned casually against the frame.

He looks so delicious that I wish I'd at least taken the time to brush my hair.

"Hi," I say, my big goofy grin leaving no doubt that I'm happy to see him.

"Hi," he returns.

We stare at each other, and I wonder if he's thinking about last night. I am. I can't look at his perfect lips without feeling the ghost of them on my own.

"Can I come in?" he asks, his smirk lifting his lips in a deliciously sexy way.

"I don't know if you should. I'm all alone," I say, pretending to be shy. His smirk turns into a deadly smile and he pushes the door open wider so he can join me inside.

"I know," he says, pulling me against him. My breath stutters before my body relaxes against his hold. God, I love the way he feels pressed against me. It's heady and intoxicating, and I have half a mind to yank him into my bed. He's so much better than room service.

"So, you came here to take advantage of me?" I ask, smiling up at him, my eyes begging him to kiss me.

"Is that okay?" he asks, his hold tightening.

"More than okay," I admit. His face drifts towards mine, and I wait for the moment his lips will brush across mine. The breath of space between us is charged with a sexual promise that I both crave and fear all for the same reason: that it will take me under so swiftly that I won't find my way out.

When our lips finally meet, my world goes hazy. I've kissed lots of boys, but his man kisses me completely, owning every second, every breath.

"You taste like chocolate," he mutters against my lips, his tongue running across them as if he needs a better taste. I feel a shiver run through my body as everything inside me clenches with want. With need. I mumble a response, but I'm not sure it consists of words and it makes him smile. He pulls back and I have to blink back into focus. "You want to hang out with me today?" he asks.

I nod, "Uh huh." My earlier plan for a lazy day all but forgotten.

"We can be tourists," he suggests.

"Give me a few minutes to change?"

"Take your time," he says, kissing my forehead. "I'll just read a book or something." I laugh as he picks up the open book on the nightstand and then scowls at the cover before mumbling, "Not this one."

After fifteen minutes, I've managed to pull myself together enough to venture out. A little dry shampoo and a quick dash of makeup and I call it good. I could get all girly for him, but I'm too excited to waste the time. When I walk out of the bathroom, the hungry look on his face says it was enough.

"Where are you going to take me first?" I ask.

"Should we start with food?" he asks and for a second I'm about to suggest he feast on me, but I keep it together and reply with a simple yes.

Miles takes my hand in his as we make our way down the hall to the elevators. I love the way it feels in mine. Like it was made to fit perfectly with mine. As we wait for the elevator, I stare down at the way our fingers entwine and the way his thumb grazes over my skin. His hands might be my new favorite thing about him.

"Let's start back at the pier. We can grab lunch there," he suggests.

I smile, "Sure, that sounds perfect."

I don't really care where we go. I just like his company. Everything about him is easy.

We end up at a pub nestled along the water and it's perfect. I can see people walking along the sidewalks, staring at the boats and the seals, people taking pictures of Alcatraz like they are holding the landmark in the palm of their hands and I can listen to the birds squawk as they dive for fish in the bay. I could stay here for hours and be perfectly content. We each order a beer and glance over our menus while we chatter on about random things. I enjoy being around Miles. He laughs easily, which brings out my silly side, but he's also perfected that lusty gaze that sets butterflies free in my stomach and makes me want to hand over any virtue I might have left and wrap it up in a shiny bow just for him.

He's the perfect blend of laid-back boy next door and suave mystery. I want to scoop him up and lick him like I would my favorite ice cream. He'd be his own flavor. I think even Ben and Jerry would have a hard time finding a label that fit him. I smile at the thought, throwing ideas around silently in my head. It's nearly impossible to find one that fits. Marshmallow Mocha Miles?

"Why do I feel like you are up to no good?" he laughs, glancing up from his menu.

"Why do you think that?" I ask, curious.

"Well, I've noticed when you're really thinking about some-thing, your eyes dart around like you're actually in a room looking through things. I can almost imagine you in there exam-ining and plotting," he says.

I laugh at his observation. I'd never thought of it that way, but he's not so far off the mark.

"I was deciding what ice cream flavor you would be," I tell him honestly.

"What?" he laughs.

I shrug, "You wanted to know. That's what I was thinking about. I was going through different combinations and throwing out the ones that didn't fit."

"And what did you decide? What flavor would I be?" he asks, leaning forward on his elbows.

"Still deciding," I admit.

"I can't wait for the verdict."

I smile, trying to pull off mysterious and sexy. "Me either. I love ice cream."

His eyes narrow just enough to let me know he caught my meaning, and I curse the blush that finds my cheeks as I quickly glance down at my menu. Damn. I never blush. I'm losing my touch.

The waitress comes over and we both order the house specialty. A giant burger with fries. I've never been one to order girly food for the sake of some guy. Especially on vacation. Who wants to try out the city's most famous side salad? Not me. If I'm going to make a memory, I'm going to make it count.

"A girl after my heart. A burger AND a craft beer? Where have you been all of my life?" he asks, raising his glass to clink with my own.

"Excellent beer is important. I enjoy trying new things. I also really like whiskey," I admit.

"You're full of surprises," he muses.

"It's the only way to be. Life is short. I don't believe in wasting time or settling."

"It's a perfect philosophy," he says.

"It's a lesson I learned early on," I tell him.

The waitress brings our food, and they were not kidding when they said their burgers were giant. I may not care about ordering lady like food, but I'm not sure I will get my mouth around this stack of meat.

I glance over and catch Miles smirking at me. "You don't think I can do it, do you?"

"I'm looking forward to the effort you're gonna put in it," he admits.

"I do like a challenge," I tell him.

Miles

I CAN'T HELP BUT STARE AT HER AS SHE EATS HER BURGER. I ALSO can't help the way my cock twitches when a bit of mayonnaise lands on her lip and her tongue sweeps out to lick it away. The act is so sensual that I can't help but wonder if she's practiced it before. Somehow, I doubt it. I don't think she has to think about being sexy. It's just who she is. It radiates from her skin, leaving a trail of stunned men in her wake.

Men like me.

I've been stunned.

I smile as I watch her and as she chews, I catch a small, unexpected blush color her cheeks as she notices my inspection. "Do you always watch people eat?" she asks.

"No. I just find you fascinating," I admit, forcing myself to tear my eyes from her and turn my attention on my own lunch.

"I'm fascinating?" she asks, sitting back against her chair, smirking at me. She likes that she has an effect on me. It's a two-way street. That blush of hers gets me every single time. I'm pretty sure it's not something that she does often. We could be dangerous for one another.

"Don't act like it's such a secret," I tease her.

"What? So, all of my cards are on the table?" she asks, her smirk hinting at trouble she could lead me towards. I'd go willingly.

"Hardly. But I look forward to figuring you out," I admit, holding her gaze. I want to lean forward and kiss her, slide my fingers through her dark hair, pull it from its hold and tangle my hands in the messy waves. Anything to touch her.

"I like you, Miles," she says quietly, and it pulls my grin into a full-blown smile. One that threatens to make my cheeks hurt.

"I like you too, Lily."

We finish our lunch with easy conversation, and then we venture out onto the streets of San Francisco. I smile as Lily lifts her face to the sky and takes in a deep breath of the cool air.

I slip my hand into hers as we walk, because it's become the most natural thing for me to do. Neither of us questions it. She doesn't seem to question anything. I like that about her. The way she just takes what's happening around her and molds it into a perfect world. Like she crafted it just for her own amusement.

Hell, maybe she has.

We walk along the sidewalks and she chatters, filling the space between us with random facts and jumping from story to story. I hang on her every word, just to keep up. That and I like the sound of her voice. I like the way it seems to dance on the air between us, lifted and spun in a perfect melody. Yes, I realize that I'm sounding like a complete loon, but it's how she makes me feel. For now, on this random city street, I'm okay with it.

IT'S EARLY AFTERNOON WHEN WE FIND ICE CREAM AND A BENCH TO people watch. She has two scoops. Chocolate peanut butter and cookies and cream because as she says, she can never decide which one she wants. Currently, we're discussing relationships. Not past relationships, but the theory of. And as with everything else, Lily has an opinion, and it's both entertaining and fascinating.

"Wait, okay, so what you'd just walk away?" I ask her, amused as she tells me how she has no time to hang around with a guy after he's gone against one of her life slash dating rules. What she calls a total red light.

"Life is too short to waste time. If I meet someone and they have some quality that is completely off putting, then why would I hang around? It doesn't make any sense. Everyone has a list of deal breakers. Don't pretend that you don't have your own list," she says. I love the stubborn look in her eyes. The way she jumps to a challenge anytime it's presented.

"Okay, let's hear about your list," I encourage. I'm very curious what things she considers an instant red light.

"Fine," she says, settling against the back of the wood bench. She pulls her knees up to her chest and takes a bite of her ice cream before she explains. "You can't be mean to animals. Or the elderly," she says simply.

I nod. "Reasonable. That would make you a complete asshole."

"Exactly," she says. "When I was sixteen, I went on a date with this really cute guy from school. He was a year older and all of the girls thought he was perfect. So, I was really excited when he asked me out. Anyway, on the way to dinner a squirrel ran across the road and instead of slowing down and letting him pass, the asshole sped up to hit him. He laughed and thought it was hilarious. Luckily, he had no aim and the squirrel lived, but

I demanded he stop the car and I got out right then and walked back home."

I can't help but smile, imagining this kick ass girl climbing out of that guy's car and stomping her way home. I lean forward and kiss her softly on the lips. "You're kind of amazing," I tell her. She gives me the blush I love so much.

"Your turn," she says.

"Those are your only two?" I ask.

"No, but they are the big ones. I think they say a lot about a person."

"Okay, deal breakers. Let me think," I say, taking a moment to ponder the question.

"You shouldn't have to think. You already know the answer, you just don't want to be an ass and say it out loud," she points out.

I laugh, knowing she's right. "Alright, bad breath. Like constant bad breath. The kind where it feels like you're kissing the inside of someone's garbage can or chewing on dirty socks. Can't do it."

She laughs as my face twists in disgust. "But what if I just had a big bowl of pasta covered in garlic? Or a giant cup of coffee? You're saying you'd leave me high and dry?" she asks.

"No. I'd eat garlic or drink coffee with you, so we'd cancel each other out. Besides, I'm not talking random, I just had coffee breath. I'm talking about throwing a handful of pennies you found in the bottom of your car's ashtray into your mouth and sucking on them all day long breath."

She laughs harder, "I'm going to be paranoid every time you try to kiss me from now on. I think I need some gum."

I scoot closer to her, my hand on her thigh, the space between us fading. "You have nothing to worry about. You taste like honey. It's the most addicting thing I've ever tasted. I could kiss you for hours." My voice drops low. Sultry. I feel the shiver that runs through her, the way her gaze lingers on me, her ice cream forgotten.

"Kiss me then," she breathes out the words just as I close the space completely. My lips brush across hers as my fingers brush across her chin. A taste, a tease before she steals every breath. I would happily kiss her for hours and as I pull her even closer, deepening the kiss, I am pretty sure I want to do just that.

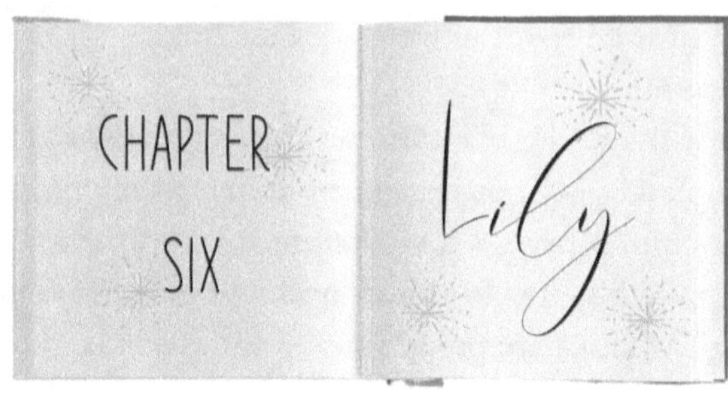

"Okay, so we've covered your first kiss and your first time, now tell me about your first heartbreak," Miles says as we walk. We've spent our entire day wandering the city. We've been to nearly every tourist attraction within walking distance, and I swear we've asked each other every question in the world.

"I haven't really had a real heartbreak," I shrug, jumping off the ledge of a flowerbed onto the sidewalk below.

"Really?" he asks, surprised.

"I'm not very good at goodbye," I admit.

"Is anyone good at it?" he laughs. He has a point.

"I'm much better at ghosting," I add, ignoring his question. This makes him pause and he throws a curious look my way.

"Wait, so you just stop calling? Ignore them until they get the hint? That's rough," Miles says.

"No, it's not that dramatic. I just fade out sometimes."

"It still sounds harsh," he says.

"I don't really do serious relationships. So, it's not like I'm breaking any hearts," I say, defending myself.

"Doubtful."

"I'm always honest. From the beginning."

"Why don't you do serious relationships?" he asks, his eyes curious as he studies me. I love the tingle that hits when his eyes roam over me that way.

"I don't like endings," I say.

"You said that before," he says thoughtfully.

"Still true."

"Not everything has to end. My parents have been married for almost 30 years."

I smile, because hard ass or not, I love to hear about the exception to the rule.

"Do you want to hear my theory?" I ask him. We're back at the pier and I stop and lean against the railing, looking out over the water.

"Of course, I do," he says. His smirk nearly makes me lose my concentration.

"It's pretty genius. It will amaze you," I tell him.

"I'm dying to hear this," he smiles.

"It's the eighty percent rule," I say. His brow furrows.

"Should I know what the eighty percent rule is?"

"Imagine life is like a novel," I explain as his head tilts to the side, trying to figure out which direction I am going.

"Suspense, romance, or fantasy?" he asks with a teasing smirk.

"Probably all, but for the sake of argument we'll stick to a romance novel We are at a romance convention."

"Fair. Continue."

"Okay, so every love story has it's beginning. Sometimes it's rocky with a whole enemies to lovers kind of thing and sometimes it all just falls into place perfectly. Instant gratification," I start.

"Like us," he bats his eyes and I laugh.

"You think you're so cute,"

"I am."

I roll my eyes and continue with my theory. "So, you've got this whole build up. You are living in the good part. The sweet spot. You may hit a bump in the road, but mostly it's easy sailing.

You are enjoying everything. You're laughing, you're riding the high of passion and anticipation. It's perfect."

"Sounds nice," he offers.

"It is. It's great. It's seductive and alluring and it just grabs hold of you. It's the lust haze, so to speak."

He reaches out and takes my hand and runs his hands across my palm, giving me the sexy eyes and right on cue my heartbeat speeds up.

"Sounds very nice," he says, his eyes locked on mine.

"Of course, it does. It's me and you. It's exactly where we are."

"Okay, so what happens next?" he asks, still holding my hand.

"Usually you settle in a bit. You get comfortable. You get used to all the good stuff. You start to count on it. Sometimes it moves from simple lust to something a little more. It grows a foundation."

He smiles and I know he's imagining it. The smile tells me that commitment doesn't scare him.

"And then 80% hits." I say, as if that should explain it all. Any reader would know.

"Keep going," he says.

"Everyone knows that when you hit eighty percent, it's all going to change. Something will happen that will take it all away. Everything that you came to rely on will get yanked away and you'll be left scarred, bare and vulnerable. It will break you. Who wants to go through that?"

"Eighty percent, huh?"

"Yep That's my cue. Leave before it all goes to shit."

"So, you ghost before you hit the deadline?"

"Yep." I say, letting my explanation sink in.

"And you explain this to all the guys you date?" he asks.

I laugh, "No. You're the first. I just let them know I'm not the girl who will be there for the long haul. I'm here to have fun. I don't need angst or drama to make things real. I'll take the good moments and hang on to those."

"Hmm."

"Go ahead, you can tell me what you're thinking."

"It's just that, if your theory is correct, then the obstacles and angst are worth it in the end because you get your happily ever after."

"Aww, but that's where fiction changes the game. Life doesn't have a hopeless romantic penning the ending. The only one writing my story is me. I'm not willing to risk it," I shrug.

"How do you know it's not worth it? You take all kinds of risks. But this is where you draw the line?" He's not dismissing my theory, only curious how I justify it.

"I guess so," I say. I don't apologize for it.

"What about the guys you date? Do you ever wonder if you ghosting out on them is their eighty percent? What if you leaving is the part that turns it all to shit for them?"

I stop, his question giving me pause. I'd never really thought about it that way before. I've always just assumed that they were on the same page. No harm, no foul. But he brings up a good point.

"Something to think about," I admit.

"I think it's a solid theory," he says. I look up, surprised. "I get the appeal. I do. It saves you a lot of heartache."

I smile, "You think? You're not just saying that, are you? Trying to stay on my good side?"

"Of course not. I guess in a way I live by the same rule. I just never realized that I did."

"It works for me," I say.

"So, how long do you think we have until we get to eighty percent?" he teases with a cocky grin.

"We already have an expiration date. We're safe," I laugh.

"It's a shame," he says, "I like you a lot. I might have broken a rule or two for you."

I don't admit that he could easily tempt me to do the same thing.

"This has been the best day," I tell him. I pull myself up onto the railing and lean out, letting the salty spray hit my face.

"Watch it, Little," he warns, pulling at my waist. I turn and look back at him, his expression worried, like he thinks I might topple over the side.

"What did you just call me?" I ask, amused.

He shrugs and then pulls at my waist again until I'm standing on the ground in front of him, looking up into the honey brown of his eyes. "Little," he confesses with a laugh. When I cock my head at him questioningly, he continues. "I was going to say Lil and it came out Little. But it fits. You're kinda tiny. I could probably just pick you up and put you in my pocket," he muses.

"Are you calling me short?" I ask, pretending to be offended.

"No. I'm calling you adorable. The best things come in small packages," I offer.

"Like diamonds?" I tease.

"And dynamite," he returns.

I laugh, slipping my arms around his neck. "I like it. You can call me Little if you want to," I say, giving him my best Thumper impression.

"But only me," he warns.

"No one else," I agree.

"Good. All mine."

I hold my breath as he leans down to close the distance between us and when he kisses me it's easy to pretend that I'm exactly that.

His.

WHILE QUINN AND I ARE STILL TAKING ADVANTAGE OF OUR DAYS AT the convention, our spare time has been hijacked by the Harris brothers. Quinn is smitten with the guy she swore was Satan, and I'm completely taken with his perfect little brother. I guess it's hard to deny a romantic fling when you're surrounded by romance.

Not only have Miles and I toured the city, but we even took ourselves on our own little scavenger hunt. Our little adventure left me with a collection of selfies of us wearing random hats, eating giant sundaes, dancing with a man dressed in foil, and Miles pushing me around a giant candy store in a shopping cart.

I love that he's up for any adventure.

I honestly don't know how I'll walk away from him at the end of this week. I wonder if it's possible to at least remain friends. Letting him drift away as a memory just seems horribly sad.

I try to push it all out of my head though. Live in the moment, the way I always do. Tonight the moment calls for dancing and the four of us are back in the club that Miles and I came to earlier in the week. I'm happy to see Quinn let loose and enjoy herself. Keaton is good for her. He pulls her out of her shell better than I can, and I've had years of practice. The two of them have been lost in their own world all night. Our double date, less double and more oh look who is in the same building. But my best friend is happy, and that makes me happy.

I shoot my new tequila shot and let Miles pull me back towards the dance floor. We're both covered in a sheen of sweat, but he's so sexy that I don't care. I'm wearing a short dress, one that hugs my curves because I want his hands all over me. My hair is piled on top of my head in a strategically messy style since I knew how hot it would be, but it's worked out perfectly because my exposed neck is like a magnet for Miles' lips.

The music throbs, the bass like an external heartbeat

pumping around us. Miles pulls me to him, moving with me, the dance a seductive prelude to everything we're dying to do in private. We've teased each other for days and we're both nearing our breaking point.

He kisses me, lips soft and commanding across my own, over my skin, around my earlobe. He kisses every bit of exposed skin. It's intoxicating. He strips away my control, begs me to hand it over. It intensifies everything I feel with him.

"You're so good at that," I admit in a voice so swooned out that I'd be embarrassed if I wasn't euphoric.

"You're skin tastes like honey," he hums across my throat. I laugh a little at the comparison.

"Sweet and sticky and like a cheerio," I muse, unable to resist. His own laugh rumbles against my chest and he pulls back, his eyes full of amusement.

"You're fucking stunning, you know that?" he says, his eyes focused on mine. There is so much promise there, so much he'll give me tonight if we give in. I'm not shy about sex. I do things that make me feel good. I do the things I want without ever thinking too hard about what it will mean.

At least I did.

Before him.

He makes me think too much.

"I want you so much, Miles," I blurt out. I didn't mean to say it, but the way the air sizzles between us, the words just fell from my lips. His eyes blaze as he tugs me closer to him.

"But I'm scared of you," I admit. I hold his gaze and watch confusion cloud his expression.

"You're scared of me?" he repeats.

"I'm scared of what I feel. It's so intense. Do you feel it? Tell me you feel it." I say. The music is so loud around us, the bodies pushing and moving like a human kaleidoscope, but it's like we are an island all our own.

"You know I do, Little," he says. His eyes are so dark, so deep with emotion, the same emotion that is pulling at my insides.

"I'm afraid I'll drown in you and I won't be able to come back up for air," I say.

"And that's a bad thing?" he asks, serious.

"It is for me. I don't drown. It's a rule. It's too hard to find the shore afterwards," I offer.

"Little, you're talking in riddles," he muses.

"Because you have me under a spell," I admit. He smiles at me and it's enough to rattle me further.

"So we'll dance then?" he asks, thankfully letting me off of the hook. For now, at least.

"I can handle dancing," I say as he pulls me closer to him.

"But just so you know," he says, his lips brushing across my ear, "You have completely enchanted me too."

By the time we leave the bar, our hair is damp and mussed, our heads foggy with alcohol and exertion. It's been one of the best nights, a memory to keep. A night full of moments worth having at any price. Miles takes my hand as we shuffle our way onto the sidewalk. The air is crisp and cool around us, and it feels nice against my heated skin.

"Should we go back?" I ask.

"Quinn is with Keaton," he says in answer, his eyes on his phone. My heart speeds up both at the fact that my best friend went back to his room and also that she left the door wide open for me to bring Miles back to mine.

"You want to come up to my room?" I ask.

His mouth lifts with the hint of a smile. "I'll take every moment you give me," he says.

I'm exhausted, yet strangely wired as I follow Lily inside her room. "I can't believe she actually stayed with Keaton," she says with the raise of an eyebrow. Apparently, it's a little out of character for her friend. But then, Lily doesn't know Keaton. My brother can convince people to do all kinds of things that they never expected to do.

I keep thinking about what Lily said at the club, about being afraid of taking things further. I get it, this feels like more than an average hook up. There is a level of connection that neither of us expected to feel. But does that mean we should walk away from it? Isn't Lily the one who keeps saying that we should grab life and all of its experiences for what they can offer? Why should we give up this one?

I've been daydreaming about what it would be like to feel her wrapped around me from the moment we met. I'll respect whatever decision she makes, but walking away from this, because we were too afraid of something real will haunt me. I'm sure it will haunt us both.

I watch her as she moves around the room, kicking off her shoes. She pulls her hair out of its hold and then gathers it back up with her fingers, securing it once again in one of those haphazard buns that make her look half messy and completely beautiful. She catches me staring and smiles she moves towards me.

"Sit with me," she offers, holding out her hand and pulling me down on the couch with her. She yawns as I pull her closer to me.

"Are you tired?" I ask.

"A little. The quiet after the chaos always makes me tired," she says.

I pull her closer, snaking my arms around her and ghosting patterns across her back with my fingertips. "I like the quiet," I say.

"Me too. At least when I'm sharing it with you," she says softly, like she's admitting a secret.

I know she feels this energy that surrounds us, the way it crackles around us. It scares her, the way her heart beats hard against her chest, the way her breath seems to depend on the next moment, the next taste. The fear of the moment it all comes to an abrupt end.

Or maybe that's me.

She shifts, her face looking up from my hold, finding my eyes as hers dart back and forth searching, debating, warring with something inside her. Then, she's moving, her hands on my shoulders as she pulls her body onto my lap, legs straddling me. She settles herself there and holds my gaze.

"Hi," she says softly.

"Hi," I return, my fingertips stroking her cheeks, running across the curves of her neck.

"What if you break my rules?" she asks softly.

"Which rules are you worried about?" I ask.

"What if we walk away and I still miss you?"

I smile, my heart tugging in my chest. There's something so sweet about knowing she feels the same thing.

I shrug, "I mean, we've still only got to be at what, 30, 40 percent? We've got time." I give her a reassuring smile.

"I think we're probably only at like ten," she says.

"Yeah, you think we got that much mileage left in this thing?" I tease.

"That's the thing, I don't feel sick of you at all," she says.

"I can promise to get really annoying. Maybe trip an old lady if it will make it easier on you."

She laughs and shakes her head before letting her hands drift to my hair, her fingers curling around the ends. It feels so fucking fantastic, the way she tugs gently as she thinks.

"Listen, I didn't expect to feel this either. We're out of our element. We're having fun. It's supposed to be easy. And it is. But I feel what's happening underneath it all. I don't know what any of it means. I know that you've told me over and over that life is short and that memories are made to be captured and held on to. I want every memory with you, Lily McCandless. I don't want to walk away with a single regret. I want to spend these last couple of days pretending like we don't have an expiration date. Like there is no eighty percent. I just want to enjoy you."

Her breath catches, her fingers grab hold of my neck, digging in, and her eyes spark with a flame that I know is about to set me on fire.

"You're right. I don't want to miss out on anything, Miles. Not one single thing. But if I get too many feelings, you may have to trip that old lady after all," she says.

"Deal." I pull her to me in an instant, crashing my mouth against hers. I don't tease her, or give her the soft kisses I have in the past, this time I take her with unbridled need and she pulls herself to me, like she can't get close enough. I know she's on the same page, barriers gone, decisions made. We've both surrendered and now we can't get close enough.

My hands find the zipper of her dress and I slide it down, letting the material fall from her shoulders and bunch at her waist. I kiss across her collarbone and down to her cleavage while I unhook her bra to release her to me. She throws her head back and moans as I take her into my mouth. I love the way she sounds, the pleasure that erupts from deep in her throat when my teeth nip at her peaked nipple.

Her hands are pulling at my shirt and so I leave her long enough to let her lift the material up and off and then we're a mess of mouths and hands again, trying to touch and kiss every exposed piece of skin.

"Take me to bed, Miles," she breathes.

I don't make her ask me twice. Standing, I take her with me, legs wrapped around my waist and I drop her to the mattress. She stares up at me, eyes wild and seductive. I stand at the edge of the bed, grabbing the hem of her dress and slide it down her body, leaving behind the tiniest pair of black underwear I've ever seen. My mouth waters at the thought of tasting her. I find her eyes and she reads my thoughts, her tongue sliding across her lips.

"Don't make me wait," she says.

"Move up on the bed," I tell her. I watch as she does, kicking off my shoes and sliding my jeans down my hips. Grabbing a condom from my wallet, I throw it on the nightstand and then I'm crawling towards her. I hook my fingers in the tiny lace and slide them down, kissing a path as I go across her stomach, her thighs. I love how she squirms in anticipation.

I don't make her wait long, mostly because I have zero patience. I'm a starving man and I feel like I've been waiting for her for forever. The first stroke of my tongue across her wetness makes her moan my name and I'm lost. I only want to hear more. I want to use every trick I've ever learned to pull every sound from her. I slide my tongue across her folds, flick her swollen clit, dip inside and taste her sweetness. I slide two fingers in and out of her wet heat while letting my tongue move across all of her most sensitive areas. Her hands pull my hair, her lips call my name and her thighs quiver against my cheeks. I want to soak her up; I want to devour her. I could stay here for hours, lost in this fog that is all things Lily.

When she falls apart, coming in violent waves I slow and let her come down before crawling up her body, settling against her and taking her mouth in a passionate kiss. "You're everything," I say against her lips.

She pushes at my boxer briefs, desperate to free me from the material that separates us. I have no complaints. I need to be inside her; I need to feel her wrapped around me. I kick them free and her hand wraps around my cock, hard and throbbing for her. She pumps it slowly, her teeth sinking into her bottom lip.

I reach for the condom, ripping open the wrapper with my teeth and cover myself. I find her eyes as I hover above her; I want to watch her, find her eyes as I slide into her. It's not a hook up thing to do, but I need it just the same. She lets me have it; she doesn't look away; she doesn't close her eyes and as I sink into her, we both know there is no way we could have walked away from this. There is no denying it. This was meant to happen.

We move together like we've been here a hundred times. There is no awkwardness, none of the weirdness that comes with the first time and learning each other. It's as if she was made just for me. "Fuck, Lily," I groan as I move faster, take her deeper. I can't get enough of her. She's perfection. Her fingers scrape across my back, her breaths coming quick. "Miles, I'm so close. So close." I reach between us, my fingers there to help push her over the edge, and when she goes, it's glorious to watch. It's enough to send me right over with her, her name falling from my lips as I cry out with my release.

I fall against her, spent in a way that has not only taken over my entire body but also every emotion. Lily had every reason to fear this. I may have to get this girl some pennies from the ashtray before this is all over.

"Well, that's definitely a memory I want to keep," she giggles as I roll off of her so she can breathe.

"Fair warning, I'm going to want to make a lot of those before our time is up," I tell her, removing the condom and tying it off to throw in the trash. I lie back on the bed and she tucks herself against me.

"Thank you, Miles," she says.

"Are you thanking me for orgasms?" I smile.

"Well, yes, but mostly for reminding me the chance is always worth taking."

Even if you pretend the expiration date isn't coming, it still shows up. It still slams into you with its harsh reality and it doesn't care when you try to bargain for one more day. We woke up this morning and the planes are still leaving town and the goodbyes are still inevitable.

The pit in my stomach is heavy, the ache in my chest is tight.

Leaving her feels like leaving the movie theater before the final scene. I'll always wonder what would have happened. Wonder what I missed out on. I have the feeling she'll always be that itch that I can't quite reach, the memory that hangs on because it was never fully resolved.

She's like a tiny hurricane. Even if I'd had ample warning, I still couldn't have been prepared for the sheer force of her. Fast and fierce, she's nearly too much to handle. But, God, it's been fun to try. Like trying to catch lightening in a jar. All of that energy and spirit in one tiny package, dark and light, pulling me in.

This past week has had my heart racing in a constant hum and I'm not sure that it will ever really settle. Even now, I can feel the electricity as it courses through my veins, like I'm on some high, some insane trip that I fear will be impossible to come down from.

I will never regret our time together. Only that it was so short.

That I can't take her with me.

I try to soak up as much of her as I can before we have to leave for the airport. Take every kiss I, so I can taste her on my tongue after I leave.

"God, you're good at that," she whispers, breathy, alluring. I don't think I've ever wanted anyone like I want her.

"I'm good at a lot of things," I tell her.

"I know," she says.

"You know a taste, Little. There is so much more on the menu," I say.

My lips linger at the delicate spot beneath her ear, and I breathe in her sigh as she shivers against me.

I wonder if we have time for a shower. I want to run the soap along her delicate lines, bury myself deep inside her as the water runs hot over our bodies. My body reacts instantly to the suggestion and I open my mouth to make the invitation as Lily moans softly, turning me to steel against her.

I'm so lost in her it takes me a moment to notice the sudden shift as Lily moves off of me. The hotel door slams and Quinn rushes in, looking flushed and frazzled. Lily rights her clothes, straightening her shirt as she sits up straighter.

"Oh, sorry, Quinn. I didn't think you'd be back so soon," Lily says, and I almost smile at how out of breath she sounds. Almost.

"I needed to finish packing a few things, and we should think about getting to the airport," Quinn says with a shrug. Lily and I watch as she moves around the room, picking up things at random. I throw Lily a questioning look and she shrugs, letting me know that Quinn's behavior is as weird as I think it is.

"Where's Keaton?" Lily asks carefully, moving towards her as she throws a suitcase onto the bed and starts tossing things in haphazardly.

"He was taking a shower. We've said our goodbyes," she says.

I'm not positive, but her voice sounds strangled, like she's choking on the words.

"Okay. Well, it is getting late. We will have to scramble if we are going to make our flight," Lily says. I don't miss the grateful look that Quinn gives her, and I feel my heart fall to the floor, knowing our time is officially done.

I watch the scene unravel around me, two friends speaking an entire conversation in between the words they say aloud. Lily moves towards me, her arm sliding across mine as she steps in close.

"What's happening?" I ask, like I don't already know.

"I don't know what happened, but it's obvious she needs to get out of here. I'm sorry," she says. This time it's me who gets the silent conversation, and it rips me apart.

Our time together, our slow goodbye, all fade into nothing as I stand helplessly watching Quinn finish packing her things. I want more time. I need more time. I didn't get a proper goodbye. I should have kissed her one last time. Taken that shower,

Done more.

Said more.

Instead, I help them with their suitcases, help them do a final room check to make sure they haven't forgotten anything, and then I'm pulling their suitcases into the hall and heading to the elevator.

Time is up.

In the rush of packing and racing down the stairs, it's hard to register that she's leaving. That I won't see her later today or steal her away for a last-minute dinner. It's funny how used to having her around that I've become, even though I've only known her a handful of days.

I say little as we make our way down to the lobby because Lily is more concerned with Quinn and the slight look of panic that has overtaken her features. I wonder what happened. She had shacked up with my brother last night and while she said they had already said their goodbyes, I can't help but wonder how that went since he's not around. Knowing Keaton, he probably fucked up and came across like the selfish asshole he can be and sent the poor girl running for the hills.

Before I know it, Quinn is sliding into the back of a cab and I'm facing the moment of truth. All good things end, and even when you see them coming, they suck.

"I gotta go," Lily says, her body so close to mine that I can feel the rise and fall of each breath against me.

"Too soon," I breathe as I brush her cheek with the tips of my fingers, hoping to memorize the way she feels beneath my touch. She gives me a sad smile and then pushes to her toes to kiss me. I cradle her face between my hands and try to let her know without a word that I don't want this to be over.

"Miles, this has been…" she fights for words, and I hear the quiver in her voice.

"I know," I tell her. And shit, my chest. It's being pulled apart and I can barely take in air. I don't take time to question what it means because she's moving to the car and giving me a tiny wave before climbing inside.

I watch in stunned silence as the cab pulls away from the curb, taking her with it.

And just like that, the quirky, mysterious stranger becomes a memory I know I'll hold on to for a very long time.

Read the end of Lily and Miles' story in
Downfall

Read Keaton and Quinn's Love Story in
On Paper

Reviews always help. If you feel inclined, I'd love if you left an honest review on your favorite review site. Thanks again for reading.

Prologue
Aria

There's something about the stale air of a hospital room, the way it hangs, heavy and still. Maybe that's why everything in it moves so slowly, why the waiting drags like sludge through a clogged drain.

How many minutes have I watched tick through an endless circle, forced forward by the long hands of the nondescript clock hanging crooked on the stark white wall? How long have I listened to the steady beep of the machines that fill this sterile room?

Hours? Weeks? Years?

Too many to count. More than enough to leave me feeling numb. Too few to heal the broken and bruised parts of me. Enough to teach me that nothing in life is guaranteed and most of the time, with the things that matter, we are helpless to control the outcome.

A lot happens when you are waiting.

When you are left with nothing but yourself and a cold hard reality.

I've learned that time shows no mercy.

I've also learned what lonely feels like. Not because I'm alone, but because I am scared.

I hate the waiting.

I hate everything about it.

Still, I'd wait forever if it meant this horrible room could save the man I love. I'd stare at this clock, breathe this air and endure the weight of it all if it meant we could have the future that we'd planned.

I'd give anything to fix this whole mess.

I watch him as he sleeps. The steady hum of the machines that surround his bed serving up a white noise that numbs me to my core. Each one sending something else to try and help his body fight against the inevitable. I find myself praying to those tubes, bargaining with each beep, each drop of medicine that maybe they can do the impossible. Maybe they will erase this whole horrid chapter of our lives.

It's exhausting.

Defeating.

But you have to lock all of that away when you walk into this room. In here, there is no room for negativity. He needs strength and if that's all I can give him; I'll do all I can to do just that.

Even with his weakening body, he still looks as handsome as the boy I fell in love with all those years ago. Even though the long sandy hair I love is gone, I have the urge to brush my fingers across his face the way I used to when it would hang in his eyes.

I don't want to wake him when he's finally resting peacefully. It's late and I'd give anything to crawl into the tiny bed with him, curl up against his chest and listen to his steady heartbeat. Right now, it's the only thing that gives me comfort.

He begins to stir, and I hold my breath waiting for him to open his eyes. He smiles and it's worth the late hour and all the waiting. "You shouldn't be here," he reprimands. I give him a bright smile and reach out to cover his hand with my own.

"I love it here," I tell him. It's a lie. I hate this place, but I love him and being with him is the most important thing to me.

"That is the saddest thing I've ever heard," he says, trying to sit up.

"Here let me," I offer. I hit the button on the side of his bed, lifting his head, then I jump up to adjust his pillows. It makes me feel better to actively do something. It helps ease the constant helplessness I constantly feel.

"Thanks, Babe," he smiles. His voice is tired, but I smile through the worry gripping my heart. I don't remember what it's like to breathe deeply. Ever since this nightmare began, I've held my breath, too afraid that one wrong move will completely topple everything. As if I have that much control. Isn't it funny how at times like this we find hope in superstition?

"How are you feeling? Can I get you anything?" I ask him.

He shakes his head and laces his fingers through my own. "Just sit with me for a bit. Tell me about your day. How was class?"

This has become our routine. He stays here and I go out and try to live the life that he left behind with his diagnosis. I do it because he asks me to do it. It's his way of keeping some sense of normalcy despite everything that is happening.

I tell him about my classes, boring chatter about my professors, the paper I'm writing for my lit class and some gossip from our circle of friends. It all feels so meaningless, but I still play the game.

If it were up to me, I'd stay in this room all day, every day. Everything outside of these walls feels like a chore I'd rather avoid. But I'm weeks away from graduating from Vanderbilt and I know that it's important to him that I keep up with my classes and graduate on time. It used to be important to me too but knowing that I'll be graduating without him takes any joy away from the achievement.

For me, life stopped the moment the doctor told us that Will had cancer. One single moment and everything I knew was different.

Everything.

Just like that, a few words and our entire future went up in smoke. The doctor spoke the words and all I could say was, *'But we're getting married'*. I hate that I sounded so selfish in that moment, but it had only been two weeks since he'd slipped the diamond onto my finger and now this man, this stranger, was telling me that I might have to give up everything. He was telling me I could lose my best friend. The love of my life. He was taking away everything and he didn't even seem to care.

The doctor had given me a sad smile and Will had squeezed my hand as he asked legitimate questions about treatment and expectations. But I was in a daze, only certain words penetrating the fog. *Stage IV, surgery, Chemo.* It was all too much.

It's been six months and the fog hasn't cleared. It's simply become my new normal. The truth is, we are playing a losing game against time. He's not responding to treatment and I know that we won't come back from this. It's that knowledge that keeps me in this room. I'm not giving up a single second if I can help it. I can't give up on him.

On us.

I met Will Henry, the boy with two first names, when I was just fifteen. I was shy and completely unsure of myself and he was the center of attention. I watched him from afar, but never entered his orbit. So, when he approached me at the home-coming dance, I wondered if I was in the middle of one of those high school movies where the cute guy is trying to win a bet by asking the wallflower to dance. But Will was genuine and when he led me out into the crowd of kids and put his hands on my waist, I forgot all about his group of friends watching. I forgot about the wide-eyed friends I'd left behind on the opposite side of the gymnasium. It was like in that one moment we became a pair, as if an invisible vine had wrapped itself around us, binding us to one another in a way we'd never look back from.

From that very first day, Will Henry and I'd become insepa-rable. The perfect picture of young, first love. He was everything to me. I grew up with him, experienced all of my firsts with him. We were the lucky ones. We didn't fade out. Time didn't pull us apart; we grew together, and we grew stronger. So, it was no surprise when he asked me to be his wife. It was the next natural step. It was meant to be.

I'd never been happier than I was that day. It was perfection. We'd had lunch at one of our favorite spots and afterwards he'd suggested that we take a walk. I had no idea what he was planning, walking along the river or through the park was normal for us. I loved to stroll along the path beneath the giant tree tunnels, holding his hand and talking about everything, big and small. That afternoon was no different. Except that on this day, as I prattled on about whether I'd take brownies or cookies to his mother's that Sunday, he was falling to one knee and asking me to be his wife.

There are times in your life when you feel pure happiness, the kind of moment when everything is completely perfect and it's like your whole life has instant meaning. It was like that. It was as if every dream I'd had was coming true in those four little words. Will you marry me. It didn't matter that we'd talked about getting married since we were fifteen, or that we'd planned our wedding or talked about what we'd name our kids. All that had been someday, and this moment brought it all into reality.

Happiness is fleeting. At least that kind of happiness is. I guess it's unrealistic to think you can hold on to it for any real length of time. It's too much, too powerful to be held onto so tightly. Maybe we were foolish to tempt fate the way we did, to expect so much like it was owed to us. To act like we deserved it. Maybe that's where we went wrong.

At least those are the games I play with myself when I'm sitting in the quiet of this room trying to sort out just how different everything is now. The happiness of that day, the weeks that followed, they seem like they belong to someone else. They are part of a different life. The life we were supposed to have.

One where hope still breathes. One where I don't have to fight with every moment just to survive it.

Will is loved. People are here every day. A parade of visitors with smiles that cover somber faces. We're all trying. Being upbeat is exhausting and as the days pass it's getting harder to keep up the charade. We're losing him and reality is setting in. I sit with his parents, his sister, I comfort his four best friends as they try not to show emotion with each visit. We're all in a waiting pattern, trying to be strong for each other, but failing when it comes to finding it for ourselves.

I've watched the parade all day and finally I have some time all to myself. These are my favorite moments. The ones where I just get to talk to him. He's been sleeping more and more, and these conversations are getting fewer and fewer. I hang onto every moment when he has the energy to talk to me.

Tonight, I see it in his eyes, the resignation, and it rips at my heart. I know him better than anyone else and I know what that look means. I know this is the conversation that he's been waiting to have and ready or not, I'm going to have to listen.

"You are so beautiful," he says, a hint of his smile finding his lips.

"You're on drugs," I tease, trying like hell to keep it light, to keep whatever he has planned away just a little bit longer.

"Come closer, I need to talk to you," he says. I release the breath I've been holding and do as he asks, leaning in and taking his hand in mine.

"It's almost time. I can feel it," he says. I feel the band aid ripping off, and the pain is immediate, stinging and sharp. His words so soft that if I weren't this close, I probably wouldn't have heard them. But I am, and they are so loud that I can't ignore them. Instantly, my eyes fill, and I try my best to swallow down the pain.

I shake my head, "I'm not ready."

"Baby, we're never going to be ready. We're losing too much to ever be ready." My eyes lock on his and I know he can see my fear. I can't hide it. Not anymore. "I'm tired, A. I'm really tired."

He's been trying to be strong for me all of this time, so I know that this confession is hard for him. I know it means he's reached his breaking point. I can see the weariness in his eyes, something he's been hiding from me for weeks. Something I chose to pretend wasn't there.

The doctors have told us he's survived longer than they'd expected. That used to give me hope, but now I realize that he's been trying to hold on for me. He doesn't want to leave me until he knows I'll be okay. But how can I ever be okay?

"I don't want you to hurt anymore," I say honestly. As much as I can't imagine losing him, I don't want him to suffer. I don't want to see this pain in his eyes, the way he tenses with every movement, the way his breath catches only to return shallow exhales.

I try my best to fight the instant tears that threaten. But he can see them. He takes my hand and runs his fingertips across my skin in an effort to soothe me. To soothe the pain from the things he's about to say.

"Every moment I've had with you has been the best of my life. I wouldn't change a thing. I only wish I could give you forever. It's my only regret," he says.

I try hard not to break, knowing he's telling me goodbye. It feels like a million icy hands clawing at my heart, trying to tear it from my chest.

"You'll always be my forever," I tell him, my voice broken.

He smiles, weakly, but enough that I can see the crooked grin that I love so much. "I wasn't meant to be your forever; you were only meant to be mine." Tears fall silently, blurring my vision as I stare at his face, looking for answers. "This isn't the end for you, Aria. You have so much life ahead of you. My ending can't be yours. Do you understand that?"

"I don't want to think about any of that. We're together now, that's all that matters to me."

He takes a deep breath, although it's weak, it prepares him to say what he needs to. What he's been waiting to say.

"Right now, you can't see it. I understand that. But I need you to hear me when I say this. Really hear me, Aria."

I nod, even though I know I won't like what he has to say. But it's not about me. This is about him and letting him find the peace that he needs.

"Don't let me be the last man to love you. Don't bury your heart with me. It's too beautiful not to share it with someone new." I close my eyes against the thought. I know better. I will never love someone like I love him. I don't even want to try. The very thought turns my stomach.

"I will never want anyone else, Will. I put on this ring and promised you my life. I meant it then and I'll always mean it." My voice is strong. He may need me to hear him, but I need him to hear me.

"You've given me everything I've ever needed. You gave me the kind of love people search their whole lives for. I had it. I don't know when it will happen, but someday, your heart will heal, and you'll be ready to let someone in. I need you to know that when that day happens it's okay to take the chance. I want you to. I want you to live a full life, with love and a family. I want you to want that too." His voice cracks as he finally starts to give in to the emotion of the moment.

"I only want that with you," I tell him honestly.

"Now. Right now, you can't see past this moment. But you will. Time will pass. You're going to heal. I need you to heal. Later, if the thought starts to whisper to you, I'm only asking you to listen. I need to know that you are going to be okay."

I want to tell him that I'll never be okay without him, but I know that I can't burden him with my defiance. No matter how hard I fight, I'm not going to win this war. If he needs to know that I'll be okay, then I have to make him believe that I will. Even if it means making a promise I'm sure I'll never be able to keep.

"Okay," I manage. I see the instant relief as he sinks into the pillows behind him.

"I love you. Kiss me."

I lean in and kiss his lips, whispering words of love in a silent prayer.

"Go get my parents and the guys. I need you all here right now."

The hammer hits my chest and the blow nearly throws me to the ground. My fearful eyes find his and I know we don't have much time left. "I love you," he says, his eyes locked on mine, the sheer power of his words hitting me full force. I can't say it back, because the reality of this moment has stolen everything from me, even my words.

Somehow, I manage to step back outside where Will's family and his four best friends wait. We've all had our time alone, our private goodbyes and now it's time for us to be strong together so that he knows it's okay to go.

I watch them all file in. His parents look haunted, his sister hugging me with matching desperation before disappearing behind them. Then, I face the four guys who have been like brothers to him his whole life. Dash. Carter. Drew. Silas. They look so lost that I want to comfort them. I just don't know how. They look to me for answers that I don't have. Answers I will never have.

"It's go time," I say, my voice flat. I'm trying so hard to hold on to any strength I can find. But there is none. I turn quickly, towards the room, afraid to meet their eyes and let them follow me into our new nightmare.

LET'S CONNECT

I love to chat and get to know my readers. Come say hi!

- Website
- Facebook
- Facebook Author Page
- Facebook Reader Group
- Instagram
- Amazon Page
- Goodreads
- Bookbub
- Spotify